PUBLISHED

A Craft Guide

Essays by

Maria Duarte, Leslie Gonzalez, A.M. Larks,
David M. Olsen, A.E. Santana, and Chih Wang

Edited by A.E. Santana

KELP BOOKS

First published in 2022 by Kelp Books, LLC.
www.kelpjournal.com/books

Library of Congress Control Number : 2022941639
ISBN: 978-1-7373228-6-3
Printed in the United States

Edited by A.E. Santana
Book and Cover design by Katarina Naskovski

CONTENTS

Foreword	1
Thoughts on Structure by David M. Olsen	7
Understanding Point of View by A.M. Larks	14
Dialogue by Chih Wang	54
Writing Believable Chracters by Leslie Gonzalez	80
The Suspense is Killing Me by A.E. Santana	104
Thoughts on Finding Your Voice by David M. Olsen	129
Literary V. Genre by A.M. Larks & A.E. Santana	134
Living With Craft by Maria Duarte	143
Acknowledgements	151

FOREWORD

"A writer is someone for whom writing is more difficult than it is for other people." ~ Thomas Mann

In my early twenties, a friend who was also a hopeful writer asked me to teach her how to write. I was confused. I honestly had no idea what she meant. When I asked her to explain, she wanted to know how to make her story sound a certain way. She wanted to know how I was able to make my characters believable, how I decided when they should say something and what they should say. She wanted to know how I was able to get from the start of my story to the end of it. I didn't recognize it at the time, but she wanted to learn craft.

This idea of teaching craft was foreign to me because I had picked up storytelling the way a musical person is able to play a song after hearing it. I could write but I couldn't explain what I was doing, not enough to teach someone else. I didn't have the language for it. I continued to write that way for a long time, knowing what was right without having the ability to explain it. I wrote that way through my journalism degree; through publications in newspapers, journals, stage plays, and anthologies; and even, funny enough, through my mass communications degree. It was only when I received my MFA, that I finally felt like I had the language to talk about everything that I had been able to do. Now I could teach, because in my MFA I learned what people meant when they said "craft." I realized that craft was a mix of specific guidelines (dialogue, structure, characterization, etc.) and abstract elements (voice, mood, tone, etc.). That combination of specific and abstract is one of the reasons craft can be hard to pin down, learn, and teach.

So, craft, the art of writing, may be better explained as the art of communication. While pushing boundaries or adhering to the standard points of craft is great either way, when telling a story, properly communicating your information to your audience should be a priority. Communication works best when the sender (writer) and receiver (reader) are both on the same page, no pun intended. Barriers to communication in writing can include unclear wording, poor structure, a nonsense plot, and unneeded dialogue. This doesn't mean that writing must be direct or linear, but it does have to be strategically consistent to help alleviate any unintended barriers so that the reader may understand what you are trying to communicate with them. Even notoriously complicated pieces like *House of Leaves* have a structure and style that is cohesive, albeit seemingly coded. Once the way the information is being communicated is understood, an originally frustrated reader may become a starry-eyed fan enamored with the craft of the novel.

Which is why learning craft will only take you so far but is still an integral part of the process. Start with the basics to help avoid making amateur mistakes—like being sure your story has a beginning, a middle, and an end.

These basics are infrastructures for communication. Readers need to be able to follow your story, so adhering to rules of, for example, dialogue, plot, or point of view, assist that communication between you and the reader. That is definitely a major reason to learn craft, but there is another more aesthetic and imaginative reason to study craft.

It wasn't until I knew the specifics of what people meant by pacing, point of view, tone, etc. that I realized I could go beyond straightforward prose and storytelling and enter experimental craft territory, like *House of Leaves*, and that my story could still make sense. The quote, "Learn the rules like a pro so you can break them like an artist," is attributed to Pablo Picasso. In that quote lies the all-important reason behind learning the rules. In understanding craft, internalizing it, you can respect the communication between you and the reader, and are then able to allow your inner creative onto the page without sacrificing the experience and enjoyment of your audience. Once the basics of craft have been mastered, you can then play with it. Now that you know your story needs a beginning, middle, and end—and why—you can ask yourself, "Does my beginning, middle, and end need to be in that order? How can I use the elements of craft to be artistic yet keep communication with my readers?"

In this book, you will find a diverse range of craft essays. There are structural how-to essays, think-pieces and musings, and even essays that fall somewhere in between. We have asked some of our current and past *Kelp Journal* editors to talk about the points of craft that they find important. For many, it was topics they struggled with in their own writing, those craft elements that they intensely studied to discover how to tell a better story. For others, it was topics that they had a knack for and, in learning craft, learned how to share that knack with others. With that, David M. Olsen discusses structure and voice in his essays. Chih Wang explains the rules of dialogue. Leslie Gonzalez explores what it takes to create believable characters. A.M. Larks examines the different types of point of view and how they work. Maria Duarte muses on living as an author and where craft fits in. I describe the process of building suspense in any form of writing, and A.M. Larks and I delve into what we think the differences are between literary and genre fiction.

This guide is assembled so that foundational writing elements, such as structure, point of view, dialogue, and characterization, are found in the first half. Components that build on these foundations, such as suspense, voice, and understanding the difference between genre and literary writing, are found in the second half with a philosophical essay on coexisting with writing rounding out the collection.

While editing the book, I noticed that there exists a common thread among the essays—communication, and the importance of it struck me all over again. I wish I had the know-how over a decade ago to communicate craft to my friend. Because I lacked the knowledge on how to communicate what I was doing, I missed out on the opportunity not only to work with her but to also push my own boundaries and learn alongside her. I now know how I would explain pacing, tension, plot, and more, and with that knowledge, I am able to break the rules like an artist. Each one of our authors, myself included, are simply trying to communicate with you how *we* write, how *we* understand writing, and that, in the end, *you* are in charge of your own craft.

Remember that while no one can tell you how to write, if you want to share your stories with the world, the best way to do that is to thoughtfully communicate your information to your audience—and there are so many ways to do that. So, take what you can from these essays, everything else can be discarded and rediscovered on your long journey of being a writer.

— A.E. SANTANA

THOUGHTS ON STRUCTURE

by David M. Olsen

"If you want to be a writer, you must do two things above all others; read a lot and write a lot. There's no way around these two things that I'm aware of, no short cut." ~ Stephen King

The structure of a story is probably one of the elements of writing I have given the most thought to. And after reading thousands of books, and dozens of craft books it has become clear to me that there is no clear answer. Especially in short form. I mean, think about micro fiction. You are telling a piece of a scene while trying to convey a larger narrative. Short stories, I once heard an editor at a major magazine say, don't necessarily have an entire five-act structure as long as they "complete the thought." If you're writing a novel, you may have more work to do than to just "complete the thought." In a novel we want to see a character end up in a new and different position at the end. Readers want to see change. And the novel is the path to that, and there are a few things I have learned that I can share on the topic.

Novels are built with building blocks: scenes. And every scene has to feel real to you, and you should fall in love with the writing every time. Be there, feel the drama, the pain, the emotion of the characters and you'll most likely end up with prose that engages a reader well. The hardest part of writing a novel though, is building these little blocks into an overall narrative that hammers home your overall goals for the work. It takes a lot of practice.

You have to hold space in your mind for where you want the book to end up, while also making each scene along the way feel tangible and carefully wrought. There are two visual roadmaps the helped me tremendously in envisioning how to accomplish this herculean task. One roadmap is Freytag's Pyramid. The other is Save the Cat Writes a Novel. I think everyone should read and study these two tools. You may not use them verbatim, but they provide a framework for you to lay those building blocks into so that you end up with a cohesive structure.

Here is the pyramid.

Isn't it lovely? Exposition in this case leads to the inciting event. But, as you will read in STCWAN, it may not be enough to just have a character in a status-quo state. It is often better if your character has a major issue, or more that one, in their current state that is preventing them from achieving something in life. Often this can be that they want something that isn't right for them, and through the process get what they truly need, rather than what they want. I know, it sounds like every romcom in history. But you don't have to be corny about it, it can be nuanced and complex. You'll find STCWAN shows you the tried-and-true methods that story tellers have been using for centuries to connect with an audience.

Now we have a character with a problem, an inciting event, and an idea where this book is headed. I would suggest first sketching out the five-act structure and taking that work and completing the beat map provided in STCWAN before you write too much. Maybe not plotting the whole book out, but you will have a good idea of where you want to take things. That leads me to the two schools of thought on writing a novel.

There are Pantsers (defined by one who writes without a specific idea in mind of where their characters will take things) and Plotters. I will say, however, that even a Pantser probably has one or two things in mind before they begin. One thing would be that they know who their protagonist will be, to some degree, and likely their antagonist. They usually have an idea, too, where the action begins, and either how it will end, or at least, an idea for the ultimate climax. I call this the seed. The idea that sparks the motivation to begin the journey of writing a short story or novel. John Updike was a single draft novelist, correcting and obsessing as he went. Stephen King is famously a Panster, uncovering his dinosaur's bones a fragment at a time. I would say that, to those starting out, the more effort you put in before you start drafting, the better your first draft will be. At least sketch out a five-act structure and build out a solid set of scenes that can tell that story in a satisfying way. Then maybe apply STCWAN to the first draft, and then dig into the second draft. The truth is, while you're reading critically, and continuing to write, you will begin to build a sort of muscle memory for how a story forms and pays off. Then, maybe you might graduate to a true Stephen King style Pantser.

I have tried both Pantser and Plotter strategies, and I can say that when I do some research, develop deep characters with real backgrounds, and at least sketch out the five-act structure, I end up with a MUCH better initial draft. Pantser writing is not for the faint of heart or mind. You can end up with 120K words that are no closer to a novel than when you started. In fact, all you may have done is learned what your novel isn't. Which can be helpful, but not a very respectful use of your time. No matter which directive you chose, when you are on your initial draft, let it all pour out. Liberate yourself from quality, or else you might have a painstakingly slow process of the first draft. I think you'll surprise yourself on how good some of the stuff is that flies out of your subconscious and onto the page. Especially with a map on where you are going.

I have written three novels (and two halves). The first two are trunk novels. And the third novel is on its fourteenth full draft overhaul. The current novel is where I am learning the most about what my needs are as a writer and am developing my own process. I think, after nearly a decade of creative writing courses, I would design and teach the following course to my starting out self.

I would ask that the writers begin by writing out the big, brilliant idea for their novel in a page or two. Then I would have them write a page or so defining their main two or three characters. I would have each of them put together a Pinterest board for each character, as well as the locations where the stories take place. Get them to visualize all of these major elements in the real world.

Then I would make them sketch out the five-act structure. The inciting event (what happened to our protagonist out of the ordinary), the rising action, the climax, the falling action, and the conclusion. Then I would have them sketch out thirty to sixty scenes, using no more than a short paragraph or two for each. Spare, no dialogue. Then I would have them apply the STCWAN beat map to the scenes and see if they need to be reworked or rewritten. We could review and workshop these preliminary blueprints and make sure they work before the real writing process begins.

I would expect that as characters interact organically on the page, that things may change along the way. But the artist now has a road map, a rule book, so to speak, and they can choose to ignore it with intent, knowing full well that the new, or old, direction is where they want it to head. It just gives the beginning novelist a greater sense of confidence that they will create a story that works. It helps the well never run dry, and always gives you a place to start.

The Art of Page Riding

Although I have written fiction from a young age, I started taking craft seriously around the same time I started surfing, almost a decade ago. What I learned is that the two tasks, though wildly different in their execution and, well, virtually everything about them, required something similar of the human mind. Surfing requires a whole new tool kit of skills that have to blend together in perfect harmony for the art of wave riding to occur. You first have to have the correct equipment. Next, you have to be able to read the ocean, understand the tides, and then you have to learn to paddle out, taking waves on the head as you do. Then you have to learn to navigate the line-up, the pecking order, meet people.

Most importantly, in order to catch a wave, you have to get yourself into the right position, paddle at just the right speed to match the wave, read the surface of the wave to get into the shoulder, know the exact timing of when to pop up, plant your feed, race down the face, and make your first turn. Your brain is making thousands of micro-calculations. And after years of practice, you start to get better, and you don't think about any of those things anymore. You think about the wave, the rush, and let the power of the moment flow through you. You are connected into something greater than yourself and thinking about anything else mars the experience. They operate in the background, like muscle memory.

Writing has had a similar learning process for me. It requires the study of dozens of different craft elements, you have to read and break down the work of others critically, and your brain slowly assimilates all of this knowledge, and allows you to turn, paddle, and take off on that page. To write in your own natural voice, and turn those words into a work of art.

George Saunders makes an argument that we all, as writers, find our voice and that it is often not the voice we wanted. So rather, our voice prevails over the other tonalities that we emulate when we first begin writing, and often well into writing. So, my two cents, study craft, learn everything you can, read everything critically, and when you write, don't try and control anything. Just leap up onto that wave, and let it ride and flow as naturally as you can. Worry about the rest in revision. But, I think, always have a clear idea of where you want things to go in a piece. Visualize it. Just as you would visualize your course down the face of a wave. Visualize your success down the page, and into your career as a writer. And remember, good writing is unexpected yet inevitable.

Lastly, have fun and meet people. One of the greatest things about becoming a writer, and being a writer, is engaging with other artists. Be a good literary citizen. Read the work of others, be kind, generous, and supportive. Build your network in this new passion. Because that will help you find joy and contentment in the process. And, as with life, the journey is the destination. So, take it all in, and never rush a single thing.

ABOUT DAVID M. OLSEN

David M. Olsen is editor and contributor to the surf-noir anthology, *The Silver Waves of Summer* (Kelp Books, August 2021). His work has appeared in *Catamaran Literary Reader, The Rumpus, The Coachella Review, Close to the Bone, Scheherazade,* and elsewhere. He attended Stanford's OWC program in novel writing and holds an

MFA in Creative Writing and Writing for the Performing Arts from the University of California, Riverside in Palm Desert. David is a former fiction editor at _The Coachella Review_ and is currently the editor-in-chief at _Kelp Journal_. He is at work on a collection of linked short stories, a novel, and a chapbook. He resides on California's central coast where he surfs regularly.

UNDERSTANDING POINT OF VIEW

by A.M. Larks

P oint of view is a comprehensive topic, and my craft essay tries to give fair play to the breadth and depth of this topic. But it is a lot. Some of it may be basic, or information that you have already encountered. If that's so, feel free to skim over to "When Point of View Goes Wrong," I won't know either way. But I always think that the best place to start any discussion is with a shared understanding of the basics.

So, I am going to start at the beginning and define point of view (POV), then I am going to move into a section that discusses how we talk about POV in the craft of writing and why we use those words. I am going to argue why you, dear writer, need to pay attention to POV, lest your reader stop reading. Then, I am going to transition into the most common POV problems I have come across and how I recommend fixing them when editing. I have designed these sections to not only provide you basic information but to also supply tools that you can return to time and time again to use in your own writing and editing. I have also pulled out and highlighted key concepts so that you don't have to search for that one quote buried in the middle of a long and droning paragraph. I am a writer, too, and sometimes there isn't time to read a forty-plus-page craft essay. I get it. I know. So, let's get our POV party started.

WHAT IS POINT OF VIEW?

POV is one of those things that we've all heard about, but it can still be exceedingly difficult to pin down. We ask others to "see things from our side" and we even teach children to "look at it from another's point of view." But what exactly is POV and how does it apply to your writing? In trying to describe POV, I have seen other authors call it the "lens" of an author's work, or the "eyes" of a piece. Some define POV more broadly and say that it relates to the "perspective" of the story. And still there are those who incorrectly define it as the "voice" of a story. But none of these metaphoric explanations nail down exactly what POV is and how it relates to the craft of writing. So, I am choosing to dispose of the metaphors and give you a straight definition. Point of view—in everyday life—means a particular attitude or way of considering a matter (which is why we teach the concept to children). In writing, however, point of view is defined as the perspective of the character that is narrating and, more specifically, it is the position from which something or someone is observed.

Point of View (in writing) is the perspective of the character that is narrating and, more specifically, it is the position from which something or someone is observed.

In short, that means every word you write as part of your story is linked to POV through narrator, person, and tense.

To illustrate this concept when I lecture, I put up a PowerPoint slide with a two-panel comic. In the first panel, we (the audience) are viewing a man stuck on a small, deserted island as though we are standing behind him. We see him joyously shouting, "Boat!" in reaction to the lone shaded figure in a boat in the distance. In the second panel, we are looking at the island from behind the man in the small rowboat at the sea. This man is joyously shouting, "Land!" as he looks at the island shaded in the distance.

I love this comic because it succinctly captures exactly what POV is. Each panel shows one of these characters' point of view, and in each one the story is different. Because each man has a different perspective, both literally (from the sea or from the land) and figuratively (from whatever got him stuck on an island or whatever got him stuck in a boat), how each man views the other's possession is altered by that man's specific circumstances and his history. The man who has been stuck on the island would celebrate a boat, and the man whose has been stuck in a boat would celebrate the finding of land. In other words, whether he values his boat, or his island depends entirely on that man's point of view.

How We Talk About Point Of View

When we talk about POV in literature, we talk about which person the author uses, the depth of that narration, and the choice of the tense because each of these relate to the character narrating the story and the perspective they are narrating from. Each of these points is important because everything in writing is done intentionally. It was designed that way by the writer. So, person, depth, tense, narrating character are choices that writers make that affect the "hows" of their story. How their story is told, how effective that telling is, and how much the reader will connect to it.

PERSON

It always bothered me that the difference between POV and narrative was not explained more clearly. It wasn't until I found out that the distinction relates to how we, as people, talk that the difference made sense. When we tell stories and talk about ourselves, we are using first person (the I/me/my pronouns). So, it would then follow that if our character, the narrator, is telling a story about them/her/himself that they/she/he would similarly use the I/me/my/mine pronouns.

"Person" identifies the specific perspective of the narrator who is narrating from their/his/her point of view. And just like in speaking, there are many iterations of person. If you are talking about what you and a group of friends are doing this Saturday, you would us we/us/our/ours. Second person is used when I am the narrator and speaking directly to the audience. The reader then inhabits the skin of the character, as I have done above. I am speaking directly to you, the reader, and the audience. And in that case, I would use the you/your/yours pronouns. Third person has a myriad of options that are based on gender identity.

They/them/their/theirs is used for characters who do not identify as male or female and therefore remain gender neutral. This is considered to be a singular "they" and is not to be confused with the third person plural "they," used when discussing large groups. To avoid confusion when using "they" singularly or plurally, make sure there is enough context for the reader to understand your use of person. "Lyric Smith is a knife wielding super spy. They graduated at the top of their class from Super Spy University." As opposed to the context for the plural use comes from the use of *s* to denote multiples whether that be Pringles or sports fans. "Those damn beaver**s**! They ate all the pudding mix!"

She/her/hers and he/him/his and are used for characters that identify as male and female, respectively. It/its is used for gender neutral inanimate object narration, e.g., what a corporation's action is: "Blanky Blank LLC has modified its policy on boring press releases in order to stop pointless killing of trees." Or what a toaster does: "IT BROWNS the bread, MOM!"

Depth

Choosing the person for your POV has to do with more than your pronouns, though. It limits the depth of knowledge that the narrator can convey to the audience. Which is, again, the same limitations found when talking or speaking. When you tell a story, you can only communicate what you know, feel, saw, or experienced, and likewise a first-person narrator is also limited. You don't know what your friend is feeling, though you may guess or suppose. Similarly, a second-person narrator is also limited to only those things within "your" knowledge.

It's third-person narration where you get a little bit of a choice. Like having the option of regular or curly fries, in third person you may choose between your narrator either being limited or omniscient. Limited third (also called close third) uses third person but has the option of closely following the feelings of a specific character in the story, scene, or chapter, although it does not speak as that character (which would be first-person narration).

> Example:
> It was a cool night in the valley, Mark was sitting at his desk plugging away at another stupid algebra problem. He hated math, especially algebra. He told his teachers he was allergic. They never bought it. But then, "Why did it always make him feel itchy?" he wondered outloud, while he scratched his forearm, popping open a scab, and dotting the sleeve of his white Muddy Waters T-shirt.

As this example (hopefully) shows you, we are seeing not only what Mark is doing but how he feels about it. In continuing the story, I would be able to zoom out and narrate the events as a regular omniscient third-person narrator, but I would only closely follow Mark and his feelings for the extent of this story or chapter.

Omniscient third is often referred to as the "god" perspective because this narrator is all-knowing and all-seeing. This use of third never gets too deep into the head or heart of any specific character, and also never shows any bias or preference toward any one character. The idea is that it never gets "too close," but maintains the viewpoint of a spectator. This type of narration may be hard to find in modern writing. It was a more popular POV in classic and canonical literature (think Tolstoy, Austen, Eliot, and Cervantes), but it is still used today.

> Example:
> The strong gusts of wind swept off the rocks on the shoreline and into town where it caused havoc and destruction in ten-mile-wide easterly stripes. It blew the widow Mulaney's under garments into Old Man Smith's herb garden. It uprooted the Zador's prize winning fig tree, which fell on Thompson's new car. Little Mae Van Ruiten's Shepard got trapped in the storm cellar of the church with the Pastor's previously feral 20-pound Main Coon, and the two together tore up all the sacrament wine leftover from the conversion of the church from Catholic to Non-Denominational.

As this example (hopefully) shows, we, the reader is looking at the events of this town in the aftermath of a storm as if seeing it from an aerial shot, like God would see it. We don't stay too long on one character's woes because it is the overall picture that is the point. What has happened to the town from the wind, not what has happened to one person.

Tense

POV also helps determine the tense used in our writing. Is this something that already happened (past), is happening (present), or will happen (future)? This also ties directly back to speaking. This is how we talk to people. You may tell your boss, "Yes, that Jones file was completed yesterday. I plan to do the Larson file tomorrow, and I am currently working on Arrieta." Tense choices have a specific effect on the reader. While past tense is a commonly used tense and tends to be the one easiest to write in, present tense can make the reader feel as if those things are happening "right now." It is nice to use for action, suspense, and tension. Future tense is hard to utilize in the English language and requires a very specific set of circumstances in order for it to work in literature. Therefore, it is rarely used. Science fiction and fantasy or literary works with large interior monologues seem to be the best vehicles for this tense.

IMPLICATIONS OF PERSON, DEPTH, AND TENSE

As you can see by now, POV has to do with not only the grammar of your story via the person and tense you pick, but also the plot. Information—and more specifically how or who delivers the information to the reader—is wholly dependent upon the depth of the narration. But there is yet another layer to POV that we haven't discussed. It's what I call the "Philosophical Layer." This layer deals with the heart of storytelling and is a bit of a deep dive into literary analysis, but I promise it's something that you already do in real life.

In real life, when a friend calls you up on the phone and is speaking in an excited tone, you—as her friend—already know that she is bursting with information that she wants to tell you. You may even know why. She got that job, her dad doesn't have cancer, her kid got into that college, or her boyfriend proposed. You automatically assume the "audience role" because she is your friend. But audience roles—in literature—have to be earned and explained. You know why your friend is calling you because you are friends, and the information she is going to convey is based on your previous knowledge within that relationship. But as a reader, you have no foreknowledge of the relationship you (the reader) may or may not have with the narrator.

Therefore, the POV that an author chooses becomes even more relevant. Why would a criminal tell a first-person account of his crime? Does he feel guilty? Defensive? Is he on the stand? Is he even reliable? This is where POV adds depth, and seeing how it's done, will teach you how you can use it. If you want to show that a criminal is sorry for his crimes in a more comprehensive and complete manner, a first-person account of the event would give you this opportunity. Like people, how the characters of your story talk and what they do allows us to see who they really are. What if the context to the confession was at the request of the narrator's family? Does it change if it's the victim's family that requests the confession, or if he only confesses because the cops pressured him? Doesn't that then change the type of language that you (as the author) would use when writing the confession? What about the tone you are going for and the tense you might use?

This type of analysis can be applied to any of the POV choices in writing, therefore, it can be a tool that you can use to your advantage. Why might the author choose to implicate the reader in the actions of the narrator by using first-person plural (we/us) or second person (you)?

We understand this instinctively in real-life conversations when our co-worker is speaking for our team, or the Coach is speaking for the organization at the press conference. But why the author would include us in this narrative is a question that hangs over the use of those types of narrations. Everything in writing is intention. And if the author chooses point of view like this, it must be because their intended audience is part of the group or team, participated in the events, and is therefore part of the narrative.

For third person, the reader asks why would the author use a god-like narrator? Are they trying to get us to look at the big picture here, and if so, why? What are they saying about crime or romance or horror or trauma or society? Essentially, which point of view you use depends on what you are trying to say. Because picking one point of view over another is saying something. So, be sure it is sending the right message because an intelligent reader will be looking at your choice and its larger, more metaphorical implications.

WHEN POINT OF VIEW GOES WRONG

I know that point of view is not as sexy as building suspense or writing dialogue, nor as fun as creating compelling characters, but it is vastly important. To illustrate this, let's use what I call the "a story is a car" analogy. Think of the oil in your car, no one wants to get their oil changed but no oil (or no-good oil) and the engine doesn't run. Likewise, when point of view goes wrong the car (the story) stops running. But you are in luck, dear writer, because you don't need a certain weight or a specific brand of oil. You don't even need to choose between synthetic or conventional. You literally just need oil in your car. All of this is my weird way of saying that to have a successful story you don't have to master point of view; you just need to avoid problems with your point of view. Because ultimately, point of view is how you, the author, talk to the reader—and if the reader isn't happy, they stop reading either because they don't know what's going on or they don't care.

Bear in mind that these two conditions can exist singly, independently, or interrelatedly in your work. They can be confused by your problematic point of view and therefore experience a lack of connection to your work, or they could just get angry at you for wasting their time. So, here's where the rubber hits the road. **If readers are not connected to your work,** they don't care about what happens; therefore, they will **STOP READING.**

If readers don't understand what is going on, they will **STOP READING.**

If readers become angered at you for pulling out of a perspective, they care about for another perspective they that don't, they will **STOP READING.**

Ultimately, if you get point of view wrong your **READERS WILL STOP READING.** Which is not what you want, or why you write.

When POV Goes Wrong:
- **Readers get confused and/or angry and/or**
- **They experience a lack of connection to your work and ultimately STOP READING.**

There are other subsets of these problems that you may have heard mentioned before but ultimately, they all lead to the same conclusion: readers who are confused and/or angry and readers who don't care about what happens in your story. So, if someone has ever said that you are "head-hopping" or if you have ever been accused of tense shifting, or any of the other common problems listed below, you have a point of view problem.

The difficulty is that Point of View problems are not easily solved. Because of the sheer scope of Point of View, it means that when there is a problem with the one you have chosen, there is ultimately a problem in every sentence in your entire piece. Point of View is that wide reaching and that integral. I have a way to rout out these problems. But just note, my methods aren't a panacea, they won't find everything. They will take a little searching and a lot of thinking you your part, but I think these tips can lead you to some answers.

How To Suss Out Point Of View Problems

There are a number of common point of view problems. But luckily, they can be easily grouped by the choice of person that you have made.

Common First-Person POV Problems

The most frequent problem that I have seen when using a first-person narrator is **including information that the narrator couldn't possibly know**. Whether it's how another person feels (without being told) or things that happened when they aren't there. Your first-person narrator limits the depth of their narration, they absolutely cannot convey information that they don't have because that information is outside of their experience or outside the timeline of the story, scene, or chapter.

Going back to the comic I described in the beginning—one man on an island celebrating the arrival of a boat, and in the second panel, a second man in a boat celebrating the finding of land. What if the second panel was instead the man in the boat saying "Ahh, darn that's Larry!" and rowing away. Is that a compelling story? Is it complete or do you have questions? Of course, you have a few questions because it doesn't make sense. How would he know that the man on the island was Larry? And while you might have laughed because the situation is absurd, you don't understand how he knows, nor do you care about the fate of Larry or rowboat guy. And if the comic went on for twenty pages, you wouldn't read it because it is not a complete and compelling story. (In this situation, a reader might also stop reading because the missing information is obscured in a twenty-page-long comic and the story is therefore confusing. Conciseness is key in these things. Don't take twenty pages to say what can be said in two panels.)

So, the solution then is two-fold. First, make sure that you are narrating in the correct point of view by asking is the problem who the narrator is?

Editing Question #1:
Ask yourself: Is your story told from the correct point of view? Would your story benefit from events viewed from another?

If we were doing this for the comic story, I would ask if the story would benefit coming from another character's perspective. Is the story of a man saved from a deserted island, or is it the story of ship-wrecked guy who finds land? Maybe the answer is both. After you determine who your narrator is, the next question to ask yourself is whether the depth of your narration is correct. Would you benefit from another type of narration?

Editing Question #2:
Ask yourself: Is the depth of my
narration correct? Would I benefit
from another type of narration?

Is your issue not *who* your narrator is but how much they know? Or, maybe, is it that you need or want the reader to feel more involved in the events? Your answers to these questions will reveal whether you need to alter your point of view person narration. If you need a deeper view of events, you may need to change from a first person to a close third and see if that is deep enough. If not, perhaps omniscient third? If you want to involve the reader more, you could go from first person to first-person plural, which allows the reader to be involved but part of a group. Maybe that's not enough, maybe second person is the answer for you. If you aren't sure or can't remember the difference in person narrators, go back to the definitions and see if one sounds better for your story.

If your answers, so far, are that you have the correct narrator and the right depth, but you still have (and need to include) information outside of the narrator's knowledge, I have a few tips and tricks.

Tip #1: Characters can't know about things outside of their lived experience, but they *can* guess, assume, observe, think, and suppose.

Let's say that you are writing dialogue with a first-person narrator, the non-narrating speaker cannot have feelings, observations, or thoughts expressed as fact. They are unsubstantiated by the POV. See the example below where the narrating character is Hank.

> Example:
> Hank was so hungry he hit the bag again, this time with his head. "Give me food," he said.
> Mark annoyed, pleaded. "Can't you just wait until I am done with yoga?"

In this example, the author (me) has shifted point of view by writing that Mark is annoyed. Mark can and may be annoyed at Hank, but you can't write it that way in a first-person narration because Hank can't **know** that Mark is annoyed, but he can observe Mark act annoyed, or think and/or assume that Mark is annoyed.

> Fix #1:
> Hank was so hungry he hit the bag again, this time with his head. "Give me food," he said.
> "Can't you just wait until I am done with yoga?" Mark asked, letting out

a big sigh *like* he was annoyed.

Fix #2:

Hank was so hungry he hit the bag again, this time with his head. "Give me food," he said.

"Can't you just wait until I am done with yoga?" Mark asked. Hank *was worried* that Mark was annoyed with him. Hank always worried about being in trouble.

Fix #3:

Hank was so hungry he hit the bag again, this time with his head. "Give me food," he said.

"Can't you just wait until I am done with yoga?" Mark asked. Hank *thought* that Mark was annoyed with him because Mark didn't touch Hank when he handed Hank his food.

Tip #2: Characters can't know about things outside of their timeline of events. They can't narrate things they don't know.

I have seen a similar occurrence happen because the author has forgotten the timeline events and where their scene or chapter falls in the overall structure. Meaning that your narrator or other characters can't know things before they know them. Things that they haven't experienced or been informed about, can't be part of their knowledge and cannot be communicated to the audience. This is a problem with all limited narrators, but is most violated in first person, which is why I have included it here. Let's look at an example. Monday morning 8:00 a.m. your narrator arrives to work and waits for her boss to show up. She hasn't talked to her boss all weekend nor checked her email. Her boss was in a car accident on Friday evening and is on life support.

> Example:
> It's nine a.m., Mr. Badia isn't in yet. That's weird. He's almost always here by nine o'clock. I wonder if he had an appointment. I'll check his book. Nope, I don't see anything written down. Huh. I hope he's alright … .. Oh, that's right, he's hanging on by a thread at the hospital because of that car accident. Man. That sucks. I guess I don't have to do anything today. So … then … it wouldn't be wrong if I binged something on Netflix, right? Cause at least I'm still *at* work, *ready* to work. I just haven't been given anything to do. Cool. Gonna watch *Criminal Minds* Season 117.

As you can see from the boring example above, the narrator can't suddenly know what she doesn't know. Even though the car accident happened on Friday evening, way before Monday at 9:00 a.m., our narrator hasn't been informed of it. She doesn't know because it is not in her timeline of events and therefore, she can't tell us.

Fix:

It's nine a.m., Mr. Badia isn't in yet. That's weird. He's almost always here by nine o'clock. I wonder if he had an appointment. I'll check his book. Nope, I don't see anything written down. Huh. I hope he's alright . . .. ***Maybe he emailed me. I'll check*** . . . ***Oh damn! He didn't but his wife did. He's hanging on by a thread at the hospital because of a car accident. Oh man. That sucks.*** But I guess I don't have to do anything today. So . . . then . . . it wouldn't be wrong if I binged something on Netflix, right? Cause at least I'm still *at* work, *ready* to work. I just haven't been given anything to do. Cool. Gonna watch *Criminal Minds* Season 117.

Now that we have added in her knowledge of the event, the narrator can now logically narrate it. She now knows what she didn't know. If you have to have your narrator tell your reader something, *you have to first make sure that your narrator has that knowledge.* If it is new knowledge, like that of a recent event or new information about an old event, *you have to show how that narrator got the knowledge* (which is what I did in the above with the addition of the email). Essentially, all first-person point of view problems come down to knowledge. Ask yourself, what does my narrator know *right now*? What don't they know? How else can I deliver the information to them? Do

I need to alter the timeline of events in order to square up their knowledge with the plot points?

Editing Question #3:
Ask yourself: What does my narrator know right now? What don't they know? How else can I deliver the info to them? Do I need to alter the timeline in order for their knowledge to match the plot points?

COMMON SECOND-PERSON POV PROBLEMS

The most common second-person point of view problem is ironic, as it is simplyusing second person POV at all. This type of narration is really, really polarizing. Many people absolutely hate it. I have heard editors say they will never publish a second-person POV piece, and I have heard readers say they won't read anything written in the second person. In addition, it is one of the hardest point of views to get right. I know of authors who have had to switch out of second person because it took away from the impact of their words. So, I say, wield your second-person narrator with care. Ask yourself if your story *has* to be told in second person. What does a second-person POV provide that you can't get from other types of narration? Am I okay if people hate this story solely because I used second person?

Editing Question #4:
Ask yourself: Does this story have to
be told in second person? Am I okay
with the loss of some readers by
using second person? What am I
gaining by using second person?

Now, after answering in the affirmative to the above questions, you are sure that you want to go down the second-person POV road despite the rough terrain, let's make sure that you are successful. One problem with second person is its confrontational manner. It's as if second person screams "Hey, YOU, over here!" Second person makes the assumption that the reader will relate to the narration. That they have been through the experience and will appreciate going through it again. One major problem is not using common-enough experiences that your reader can relate to, this can be especially true because the reader is the character in second person. So, there is a disconnect if the character in the story and the reader have not had the same experiences. A first date going bad, is super common but riding an elephant while naked through a river, not so much. So, make sure that the premise of your story is relatable. The problem is a reader will stop connecting to the work if they can't relate to the things that they supposedly do in the story. A classic example of second person, (that everyone cites, raves about, and gushes over) is Jay McInerny's *Bright Lights, Big City* (1984), and one of the reasons that it is so successful is that many people can relate to the partying lifestyle, being disillusioned by your work life, and obsessing over an ex. Second person works in *Bright Lights, Big City* because, yes, we have actually done those things that the narrator is telling us we have done.

Editing Question #5:
For second person only. Ask yourself:
Is this a common-enough experience
that my reader can relate?

Tip #3: Hide the second-person pronoun as much as humanly possible.

One of the things that happens when you write in second person is you end up using the word "your" (or yours, yourself) a lot. There is no way around it because you are substituting the pronoun for a name, and you also have to use it for a pronoun. So, you end up using both where you would use a pronoun and where you use a name. (Notice how many you's were in those sentences. Ick!) The problem with "you" is that it doesn't fade into the background like the other pronouns. It sticks out like a sore thumb and basically screams at the reader. Let's look at some examples and how editing away the "you" makes it less like nails on a chalkboard and more like a symphony.

Example:
You step foot on the sidewalk outside
your apartment looking for your shoes
and you almost step in gold-flecked puke.
Hey! Weren't you drinking Goldschläger
last night? It's your favorite. You

remember you forgot your shoes at your best friend's house when Homeless Harry tells you that your feet look rough and offers you back the cowboy boots you gave him last week.

Too much "you," right? The solution is to take out as many you's as humanly possible. Here is one edit that does a fair job at eliminating the repetitious pronouns.

Fix #1a:
You step foot on the sidewalk outside your apartment looking for your shoes and almost step in gold-flecked puke. Hey! Weren't you drinking Goldschläger last night? It's your favorite. At the corner, Homeless Harry tells you that your feet look rough and offers you back the cowboy boots you gave him last week. Your shoes are probably at Slyvie's house.

But this version is better.

Fix #1b:
Stepping bare foot on the sidewalk outside your apartment, avoiding the gold-flecked puke (from last night's Goldschläger), you are on mission to find your shoes. Homeless Harry is at the corner, saying your feet look rough and offers to return the cowboy boots you gave him last week. Slyvie's house, that's

where they probably are, the shoes.

Once you have set up the "you," it is implied. The reader will understand that the narrator is talking in second person when talking about who is hungover. So, you don't need to use the pronoun as much. This little tidbit is something to keep in mind when editing and will help you get rid of as many you's as you can.

Tip #4: Have some humor.

It has been my experience that to make a second-person POV work you need to have a little humor. By this, I mean to add anything that makes one smile: absurdity, silliness, strangeness, shocking events, witty observations, satire, facetiousness, a wry tone, really anything type of "humor" is game here. The reason this works is perhaps something to do with the tediousness of the grammar (all those yous) being lightened by the content. Or perhaps if you can make someone laugh, they really do forgive you of almost anything, I am not completely sure the reason. But every successful second-person POV story I have read has had a fair amount of humor in it.

Looking back at my examples above, in the original version the comedy was there but we, the reader, were too distracted by all the you-ing to really see it. Why are my shoes at Sylvie's house? By the time we get into the third version, the humor is shining bright and clear, and we almost forget that there were any you's used at all. I've used two of them. But they don't stick out anymore. They blend right in. Humor is your friend when writing in the second person.

Close Third-Person POV Problems:

One of the problems that occurs most often with this point of view is a lack of transitions, meaning that you can't just jump from super zoomed out to super zoomed in (or vice versa) without giving your reader whiplash. You have to walk your reader through the stages, in other words, transition them to the point of view that you want to narrate from.

Example:
There was a house in a town in the world.
Peter was making scrambled eggs and
screwing it all up, like always.

Think of your reader as following the author along a path made up of your words. They go where your words take them. In the first sentence in the example above. We start small at a house, we go bigger to the town, and even bigger to the world. The second sentence starts again at the small level with Peter and his actions. There is no transition from "the world" where we left off in sentence one to "Peter" in sentence two. As you can see in the sentence below, I have added in that transition, and now the reader is not getting jerked around by the narration. There is a smooth changeover from big to small. If we go back to our "a story is like a car" analogy this would be akin to shifting through the gears. You can't go from first to fourth without going through second and third. You don't have to stay very long in those gears, but you do have to shift into them to get to the next one.

Fix:
There was a house in a town in the world
and in that house was a man named
Peter ***who at the moment*** was making
scrambled eggs and screwing it up, like
always.

This problem with transition occurs not only on the sentence level but also on the paragraph level and on the chapter level and is a bit unique to close third. This is because in close third, you can narrate both omnisciently and from a character's head. Therefore, you have to transition your reader into the depth of the point of view that you want to be narrating from. So, make sure to ask yourself, what was the depth of the narration in the last scene? What is the depth of the narration I want now? Have I transitioned my reader to it? Obviously, this only applies if you want to change the depth of your narration. If you ended the scene, paragraph, or chapter with close narration and you want to go wide at the start of the next one, you have to walk your readers there.

Editing Question #6:
For close third only. Ask yourself:
what was the depth of the narration
when I left off? What is the depth of
the narration I want now? Have I
transitioned my reader to it?

In *Wonder Valley* (2017), Ivy Pochoda showcases

her deft use of her ability to transition the reader. In one particular masterful example she transitions the reader at both the sentence level and the paragraph level and transitioning descriptions that move from person to person. She starts with a description of things a person can get used to "the heat," "ammonia smell of chicken." Then smoothly transitions into things they cannot get used to, like "the goat-eyed stares of the other interns . . ." and, finally, she moves on to describing people, "Britt's skin had already turned nut brown, not quite the terra-cotta hue of Cassidy's and the twins, but close."

Pochoda takes the reader from zoomed in (we are looking at the dirt and how it smells) to a little farther out (up close and personal with the people), and then even farther out (the surrounding land as viewed from a distance), and at last we end up looking down on the characters from above, as if we hadn't just been down there with them. Pochoda's uses transitions beautifully from sentence to sentence and then from paragraph to paragraph (she also does this from chapter to chapter) to give her readers both a close intimate view (I mean, we know how things smell) and an overall view of the events.

As a side note, if you read *Wonder Valley*, this part is a great example of the use of the second-person POV as Pochoda also uses second person in the first paragraph. She hides her you's by using the saying it once and using that implication by listing the narrator's observations after. She also uses a bit of humor (crappy wine, cheap weed) to get away with the dip into a second-person point of view and before transitioning into limited third.

Tip #5: Transition your reader in and out of your narration

using a parallel real-world mechanism.

Transitions can be hard, so it can be helpful to find a real-world mechanism that helps smooth the bumps in writing. Think of the things in your life that allow you to zoom in or out. Doesn't TV do that? When you watch a news program it allows to focus on the events around the word—giving you a wider view. Flying in a plane also changes your ability to look at the landscape by giving you a chance to view it from above. The same can be said for your characters. Trains and planes. TVs and cameras. Binoculars. Telescopes. The list goes on. We stare closely at pieces of art in museums and when handling precious items. If you are having trouble transitioning your reader to the appropriate view, make your narrator do something that mimics the transition itself. Need to see wider? Have them fly above their town and realize that the local park looks like Mrs. Pac Man when seen from above. Need to view closer? Have the witness be a birder looking through their binoculars for the rare Yellow Bellied Nesting Shooter when they see the crime take place.

Anothercommon problem that occurs often in close third narration is head-hopping. Head-hopping is when the author switches the character narrating in the middle of a scene. It causes reader confusion and frustration because they were grooving along with one narrator only to be switched abruptly to another character midsentence, midparagraph, or midscene.

Example:
Alejandro watched his *abuela's* hands

move quickly from the bowl of dough and to the hot skillet and back again. He couldn't believe she was almost ninety. She handed him a plate loaded high with pastries and stared at him. Abuela thought that Alejandro was too skinny. She could see every bone in his knobby knees through his tight blue jeans.

As you can see, we were grooving along with Alejandro, feeling all the love and respect he has for his grandmother, when we are jerked out of that perspective and now have to suddenly adjust to *Abuela's* thoughts on Alejandro and it ruins our emotional connection to the story. When editing, ask yourself if all the information is delivered through the same point of view or from the same narrating character.

Editing Question #7:
For close third only. Ask yourself: Is
all of the information in this scene
delivered from the same POV or from
the same narrating character?

It also helps the reader if you only switch the narrating character when there is a clear scene break so that the reader knows there is a transition coming, like a shift in setting or chapter break. So, to fix my example above I can either remove the offending text altogether or put this information into the narrating character's perspective. Note that is very similar to the solutions I referenced above for the first-person POV problems as Alejandro can only narrate what he **knows, guesses, assumes, observes, thinks, and supposes.**

> Fix:
> Alejandro watched his *abuela's* hands move quickly from the bowl of dough and to the hot skillet and back again. He couldn't believe she was almost ninety. She handed him a plate loaded high with pastries and stared ***at his legs***. Alejandro ***knew she thought that he*** was too skinny. ***It felt like she could see*** every bone in his knobby knees ***right*** through his tight blue jeans.

Tip #6: Use setting as a way to transition your reader from one narrator to another.

When using multiple narrators, it is helpful to the readers to tie that narrator to a specific setting. Let one narrator be looking at Boston, and the other at New Orleans. Let one love the high-desert cacti, and the other hate it. Let one drive, and the other run. That way the reader will never forget whose narrating. The easier and quicker that your reader can identify the narrator, the easier the shift and the less confusion or frustration they will have.

Omniscient Third-Person POV Problems:

Omniscient third has two main problems that stem from its god-like view on the story. As you may have already realized, the benefits of each type of narration are also the things that cause problems. With omniscient third-person narration, readers can feel too distant from the characters. Even though, technically, when using third-person POV, the writer may get into any character's head, if the writer decides to stay at a distance, to avoid the problem of head-hoping, readers can feel a lack of connection to the story because the events are observed from so far away. The characters in the story may not feel real because there isn't the same in-depth narration of feelings, opinions, and observations that one gets from a close-third POV. Ask yourself: do I need to maintain a distant view of the events of this story? Does it help make my point if the narrator is outside this world looking in?

Editing Question #8: For omniscient third only. Ask yourself: Does it help make my point if the narrator is outside this world looking in? Do I need to maintain a distant view of these events?

If you have answered yes. The solution to the omniscient narrator problem is a bit tricky. The answer, unfortunately, is to do all the other stuff really well. Without point of view to provide that easy connection, all the other literary devices have to do that for you. That means the premise, the character development, the dialogue, etc. have to convey what would normally be conveyed via the in-the-head-of-the-character narration. The reader will now only get to know the characters through their actions, reactions, and words. Examples of this style include *A Hitchhiker's Guide to the Galaxy* (1980) by Douglas Adams and the 2008 short story "Last Night" by James Salter.

Tip #7: Omniscient narrators have to have a distinct voice that looks at the event from a distance.

I like to think of omniscient narrators as judges. I've heard other authors describe them as historians or sociologists. But the gist is they are people who are looking at the events that happened and rendering their opinion on such events. Which is why they need to have their voice distinct, and why you also need to have an idea of who would be narrating this and why. What are their beliefs and alliances? It's not that you even have to let your audience know these facts, but you should be sure in order to maintain a consistent voice. Is this a robot-cat historian narrating from far in the future (which I imagine has a snarky voice), or is it a sociologist in 2025 just trying to figure out what the hell happened in 2020 (which I see having a more academic tone)?

It also seems relevant to note that omniscient narration works are often published in the literary, crime, horror, and sci-fi genres but I think this narration would work well for many genres too.

COMMON POV PROBLEMS THAT APPLY TO ALL POVs

There are few problems that apply to all the points of view. And the first is when the author does not maintain a consistent point of view and tense shifting.

Inconsistent POV

Whatever point of view you choose, you need to make sure that you do not inadvertently shift out of it for the entirety of the scene, story, or chapter. First and limited third person are really close, and all it takes is a slip of a pronoun to conflate the two. It can be hard to remember that you can't dip into everyone's head in limited third. When editing ask yourself if you remain in one point of view until your scene break, story finale, or chapter ending.

Editing Question #9:
Ask yourself: Do I remain in one point
of view until my scene break, story
finale, or chapter ending?

Like with head-hopping, shifting types of point of view narration causes whiplash to you reader, such as beginning a story in second person only to shift into limited third person halfway through. If you needed to switch in the middle of a story, was it even the right point of view to begin with? Often the answer is no, it was not.

Tense Shifting

As with problems with inconsistent point of view narration, it is easy to shift tenses when drafting. That's why when editing you need to make sure that you are not changing back and forth. Sections of dialogue and scenes where you shift the timeline of events, like inserting a flash back, are common areas where slips happen.

Editing Question #10:
Ask yourself: Am I using a consistent tense throughout my narrative?

LENGTH OF NARRATION

Another common problem that can occur with point of view is determining the length of narration. This idea is mainly applied to the least used points of view: first-person plural, second person, and omniscient third person. First-person plural and second person are hard to maintain in a book-length work without shifting into the commonly found problems. Omniscient third person can be difficult to execute in the short word count of a short story. So, it is generally recommended that you avoid these types of narration for the lengths mentioned above. But I am not a fan of hard and fast rules—and, of course, there are exceptions for every rule. Joshua Ferris in *Then We Came to the End* (2007), uses first-person plural for a majority of its 385 pages. As mentioned above, *Bright Lights, Big City* is a novel in the second person. And James Salter used an omniscient third-person narrator in "Last Night." So, I think it's okay to bend the rules and go against the recommendations, but you need to know what you are doing, and you have to execute perfectly.

**Editing Question #11:
Ask yourself: Can I sustain this
narration for the length of my
intended story? Does this type of
narration match the length of the
work I am writing?**

And speaking of sustaining your narration, I am now, finally out of POV problems. That's it. You have made it through all of the ways that POV can go wrong. But what about when POV goes right? Or really, right?

WHEN POINT OF VIEW GOES RIGHT

When POV goes right, you don't notice it. It's like when the trains or buses run on time. That's how it is *supposed* to go. When you fall in love with the characters, are compelled by the plot to see what happens next, marvel at the beautifully described settings, *feel* the dialogue, that means the POV has done its job, it has stepped out of the way and let those other elements shine. You will know when POV goes right, when you don't notice it, like the screws holding together your computer or holding up your pictures.

However, there are some authors whose use of POV rises above its role as supporting actor/actress to take the lead as the principal literary device driving a story. What these authors do is use point of view in such a way as to alter how you receive the information provided in the story.

Take F. Scott Fritzgerald's *The Great Gatsby* (1925) for example, the narration is designed to skew your reaction to the characters and their actions. Have you ever considered how biased the information that you are receiving is? It isn't a straight third person narration, *The Great Gatsby* is narrated through Nick, who has his own opinions and observations about the people involved. But as a reader you forget that and start to believe the same as Nick, you instantly hate Tom; you are sort of in love with Daisy and are in awe of (and then consequently pity) Gatsby.

Elizabeth Strout is another author who deftly wields POV. In *Olive Kitteridge* (2008), a novel with shifting points of view, the idea behind her POV use is the antithesis to Fitzgerald. Instead of skewing a reader's reaction, she widens it. The rotating POV's (and timelines) are the only way that you can get the "complete" picture of a single character, in all her glory and shame. POV of is used to convey an overall message; people are complicated. Decide for yourself who Olive Kitteridge really is.

While I mentioned *Bright Lights, Big City* earlier, you might also want to check out *Then We Came to the End* by Joshua Ferris. The second person ("I") and the first-person plural ("We") both strive to make the reader feel like they are part of the narrative. In second person though, the reader is the character and in the first-person plural, the reader is part of a group. Ferris' accomplishment is noteworthy not only because he uses first-person plural for a majority of the novel's three hundred eighty-five pages but also because he elevates the use of POV to the metaphoric level. To get the reader to compare the collective to the individual through the switching between first-person plural and omniscient narration.

When talking about first-person plural, I would be remiss in not mentioning the 1930 short story "A Rose for Emily" by William Faulkner. How is it that you as the reader feel like you did wrong by Emily at the end of the story? Point of view, that's how.

One of my favorite examples of the use of POV in a short story is "Orientation" (2011) by Daniel Orozco. There is one paragraph that he cycles through three points of view in one sentence all while maintaining the plot, the tone, and the humor. If nothing else, read it just so you know what is possible.

Variations in point of view are not limited to fiction, though that might be your assumption. Annie Ernaux, whose recent memoir, *The Years* (2017) is told in both the first-person plural and the second person and is a wonderful example of how POV can be used to give both personal and historical context. Yes, the events happened to her, but they also happened to women of her generation, they happened to people of France, they happened to people everywhere. So, it is both individual and collective. Small and wide. And thus, the POV reflects this.

Then there are the authors I fangirl about. Kelly Link and Ursula K. Le Guin are a couple. More authors who showed me what was possible with POV. In Kelly Link's 2016 collection *Get Into Trouble,* there are two stories that use POV in a similar fashion, they are "I Can See Right Through You" and "Secret Identity." In these stories, Link has her first-person narrator also talk in the third person about themselves, which essentially creates a whole other character due to the split persona of the first-person narrator. In "I Can See Right Through You," the alter-ego is the "demon lover" the actor narrator's most famous role (*Twight*-esque). The narrator is detached from his other side and narrates the demon lover's actions as though they were not his own. In "Secret Identity," the teenage narrator is more self-aware than she would life to be (ironically) and therefore she chooses to narrate the story from the third person all as she tries to pen a letter to the adult man subject of an illicit hotel tryst. The POV reflects the narrator's need to craft the right story and distance herself from her own actions.

Ursula K. Le Guin has a story called *"Ether, OR"* in her 1996 collection *Unlocking the Air* and in it she does something I have never seen before in a short story. The story is about the town of Ether, Oregon which may lead you to think that she would use an omniscient POV, but no! The story is told through thirteen alternating close third POV's of the town's residents. How Le Guin made a close third feel like omniscient third, I'll never know. And to top that off, Le Guin does what you are not supposed to do head-hopping. Somehow, she pulls the whole thing off flawlessly as only she can do.

The above list of righteous uses of POV is nowhere near comprehensive. I am sure there are many more examples of authors who made and make POV do the unthinkable, but the above gives you a good starting place to read up on POV. What I hope, now is that you will go out an make your own list. What is your favorite use of second person or first or third? Which author made you do a double take and exclaim "I didn't know you could do that with POV!"?

CONCLUSION

Ultimately, what I hope you take away from this essay is that point of view is not as scary as it sounds. That there are some easy fixes to a number of common problems. That POV doesn't have to be a big hang up when you edit.

Most of all, I wanted you to know that if you really want to get crazy on a Friday night, that you can take POV out for a spin and let her loose on your pages and see just where she'll take you. Maybe to a new metaphor. Maybe a whole new genre. Maybe a new story. Or maybe just back to the safety of the familiar. There aren't hard and fast rules like, you can never do X with POV if you write short stories, or if you write in this genre, you can only use a certain POV. Writing as we have discussed is about intention, and the above knowledge should give you all the tools you need to draft and revise your work with that intent, but art is also about experimentation. So, what I am saying is: now that you know, go play around and see what you come up with.

ABOUT A.M. LARKS

A.M. Larks writes fiction, nonfiction, children's literature, and drama. Her writing has appeared in *Scoundrel Time*, *Assay: A Journal of Nonfiction Studies*, *Five on the Fifth*, *Charge Magazine*, and the *Zyzzyva* and *Ploughshares* blogs. She has performed her stories at Lit Up at Town Hall Theatre in Lafayette, California. She is the current photo editor and blog editor at *Kelp Journal*, a multimedia literary revue, and the former fiction editor at *Please See Me* literary magazine as well as the former media editor of *The Coachella Review*.

A.M. Larks earned a Bachelor of Arts in English Literature, a Juris Doctorate, and most recently a Master of Fine Arts in Creative Writing and Writing for the Performing Arts from the University California Riverside Palm Desert's low-residency program. She is a longtime patron of the arts and enjoys stories that capture the complexities of life on the page or screen.

References

Adams, Douglas. 1980. *A Hitchhiker's Guide To The Galaxy*. 1st ed. New York : Pan Books.

Ernaux, Annie. 2017. *The Years*. Translated by Alison L. Strayer. New York : Seven Stories Press.

Faulkner, William. 1930. "A Rose For Emily." *The Forum*, April 30.

Ferris, Joshua. 2007. *Then We Came To The End*. New York : Back Bay Books.

Fitzgerald, F. Scott. 1925. *The Great Gatsby*. New York : Charles Scribner & Sons.

Le Guin, Ursula K. 1996. "Ether, OR." *Unlocking the Air*. New York : Harper Perennial.

Link, Kelly. 2016. "I Can See Right Through You." *Get Into Trouble*. New York : Random House.

Link, Kelly. 2016. "Secret Identity." *Get Into Trouble*. New York : Random House.

McInerney, Jay. 1984. *Bright Lights Big City*. New York : Vintage Books.

Orozco, Daniel. 2011. "Orientation." *Orientation and Other Stories*. London : Faber & Faber.

Pochoda, Ivy. 2017. *Wonder Valley*. New York : Ecco.

Salter, James. 2005. "Last Night." *Last Night*. New York : Vintage.

Strout, Elizabeth. 2008. *Olive Kitteridge*. New York : Random House.

DIALOGUE

by Chih Wang

THE FINE BALANCE OF REALISTIC DIALOGUE

Dialogue, when used right, can reveal something about your characters or move your story forward, or both. It's about picking and choosing the most important parts of the conversation to show the reader, and not boring them with the rest. In other words, ask yourself, what is the purpose of the conversation to your story? Is it to show conflict? A revelation? After the conversation has ended, what consequences will there be for your characters, your plot? How will it change your reader's perception of them?

There is a fine line you want to walk between dialogue that sounds too realistic and too fake. Try listening to your friends talk to each other. Maybe—with their permission, of course—record their conversation and then transcribe it. You might notice that people lose track of what they're saying and go off on tangents. They sometimes cut each other off or avoid directly answering questions. They sometimes don't say what they really mean—subtext—which can add another layer to your scene. They may talk differently to a close friend than an acquaintance, a love interest, an authority figure, a child, a parent, a frenemy, a full-on enemy, etc. They probably repeat themselves and use fillers like *uh* and *um*—more so when they're nervous. As the writer, you are the one who distills and curates the essential parts of the conversation. Do you need every *uh* and *um*? Or will they end up being tedious for the reader to read:

"I . . . um . . . uh . . . I don't know—what was I saying? Oh, wait, yeah, maybe . . ."

You can condense this to just one or two fillers for flavor and still show your character hesitating, confused:

"Um . . . I don't know. Maybe . . ."

Or even shorter:

"Maybe . . ."

For every extraneous filler, you're slowing down the pace of reading. Do you want to do this on purpose and perhaps risk losing your reader's interest? Or is this to build suspense before a momentous decision? Is the hemming and hawing to show your character is an indecisive person? If you're having every character speak like this simply to make your dialogue more realistic, this will probably become annoying for most readers.

In a similar vein, if your character has an accent, you do not need to replicate it phonetically—unless you are as skilled and as knowledgeable as Mark Twain, it is probably best to avoid it. For example, in a French accent, it can be distracting for the reader to constantly adjust to *ze* for *the* and *zat* for *that* and dropping the *h* in front of words like *hideous* for *'ideous*. It is less distracting to just tell the reader upfront that a character speaks with an accent. You could describe an accent like Joe Hill does in his novel *The Fireman* (2017), published by Gollancz:

> . . .an English accent distracted her and lifted her spirits. She associated English accents with singing teapots, schools for witchcraft, and the science of deduction.

Or you can research common foreign words, slang, and colloquialisms to sprinkle into your dialogue, enough to give the reader the *impression* of an accent rather than striving for a hundred percent accuracy. This can also work for characters speaking in languages other than English. In Silvia Moreno-Garcia's *Mexican Gothic* (2020), published by Del Rey, her characters sometimes speak in Spanish. The text is in English, but she inserts Spanish words:

> You know about the mal de aire? Your mama ever tell you about that in the city?

The term *mal de aire*, which means bad air, is a specific Mexican term used to describe the belief that breathing in cold or nighttime air causes pain or cold-like symptoms. The title *mama* is also what Mexicans often call their mothers. Americans would more likely use mom or mommy or mother. Note how the rest of the dialogue has nothing else unusual in vocabulary or sentence structure. Those two terms are enough to give the sense of a foreign language being spoken.

Avoid eye dialect, which is deliberately

misspelling words that the character would pronounce correctly, such as *yew* for *you* or *enuff* for *enough*. It is called eye dialect because you see—not hear—the word differently. Eye dialect misrepresents the speaker as uneducated, stupid, etc. and can be considered pejorative and condescending. Show accents through diction (word choice), syntax (word order), and local expressions—not spelling.

On the sentence level, another way to lose your reader's attention is showing transactional dialogue. For example, let's say there's a lunch scene during which you want one of your characters to announce a life-changing decision:

> As soon as Shannon slid into the booth, the server came by again.
>
> "Hi! I'm Emily. I'll be your server today. Are you two ready to order?"
>
> "Yes," Shannon said, "I'd like a pastrami sandwich."
>
> "What kind of bread would you like that on?"
>
> "Rye, please."
>
> "And for you, sir?"
>
> "The chicken club on sourdough," Seth said. "Thanks."
>
> After the server took their menus and left, Shannon said, "Sorry, I'm late. How's it going?"
>
> "Not bad," he said. "I quit my job. I'm going to write full-time."

The food order isn't necessary to move the story forward. One way to strengthen this scene is to make the food order reveal something about the characters:

> As soon as Shannon slid into the booth, the server came by again.
>
> "Hi! I'm Emily. I'll be your server today. Are you two ready to order?"
>
> "Yes," Shannon said, "I'd like the panang curry with duck and a Thai iced tea."
>
> "What level of spiciness?"
>
> "Zero, please. I can't handle anything spicy."
>
> "And for you, sir?"
>
> "The red curry with chicken," Seth said. "Level five—no, give me the spiciest you've got!"
>
> After the server took their menus and left, Shannon cocked an eyebrow. "You're living dangerously today."
>
> "I quit my job," he said. "I'm going to write full-time."

Even before Seth breaks the news, increasing the spiciness level hints at a change in him. Conversely, Shannon's inability to handle any spiciness hints at how she might be the type of character that plays it safe. Alternatively, the order scene can be quickly summarized with something like:

> Fifteen minutes late, Shannon slid into the booth, and the server promptly took their orders. He waited for the server to leave before saying, "I quit my job. I'm going to write full-time."
>
> "Okay, how did Rene take it?"
>
> "I haven't told him," he said, "and I don't plan to."

We bypass any small talk and extraneous information to go straight to the heart of the conversation: Seth is changing careers. This is new information that moves the story forward. The dialogue also reveals potential conflict: he's hiding a secret from Rene.

In terms of dialogue content, be careful not to use dialogue to explain information for the sole edification of the reader. In other words, don't have characters tell each other things that they already know:

> "He's going to find out," she said. "Rene is your boyfriend and has been living with you for the last three years."

This is unrealistic exposition. Of course, Seth would already know his own relationship status and living situation. There is no natural reason for Shannon to explain this back to him. This exposition only benefits the reader, not the characters. A way to fix this is to place the exposition outside the dialogue:

> "Rene is going to find out," she said.
>
> He sighed. Shannon was right. Rene lived with him. He was going to notice the absence of a regular paycheck in the mail. And they had just celebrated their three-year anniversary last weekend. Why was Seth so afraid to tell him?

Another fix is to call out the exposition:

> "He's going to find out," she said. "Rene is your boyfriend and has been living with you for the last three years."
>
> "You don't think I know that already?" he said.
>
> "Sorry, I just don't know how you

could think you can keep something like that from him."

Or to have Shannon ask for clarification:

> "He's going to find out," she said. "I mean, he's still your boyfriend, right? And how long have you two been living together now? Two years?"
> "Three," he said.
> "Right," she said. "How could you not tell him?"

Note here that the word *not* is not italicized although you most likely can hear in your head Shannon saying, "How could you *not* tell him?" Be judicious in using italics to emphasize words. Having less italicized words in the text means that when a word is italicized, it carries more weight. In other words, a lot of italicizing dilutes their impact on the reader. Besides, the reader oftentimes can "hear" the emphasis without needing to see it italicized. A rule of thumb is to italicize words that are unusually stressed.

Another pitfall to avoid is unrealistic direct address, which is when characters are addressed by their name (e.g. "Hi, Chih!"). If you pay special attention to real-life conversations, you'll notice that we rarely speak the name of the person with whom we're talking. General rules of when direct address is appropriate are when trying to get someone's attention or trying to emphasize a point:

> "Leslie, watch out!"
> "Who peed on the rug? Was that you, Daisy?"

Used too often, direct address can read like it is there only to help the reader keep track of who is speaking:

> "Leslie, this chicken mole is delicious."
> "Glad you like it, Chih!"

Without direct address, this bit of dialogue sounds more natural:

> "This chicken mole is delicious," I said.
> "Glad you like it!" she said.

Here, the reader can keep track of who is speaking by the dialogue tags, *I said* and *she said*.

So far, most of the dialogue shown are examples of direct dialogue (sometimes called dramatic or real-time dialogue). Showing the exact words of what your characters say is probably as close as you can get to having your scene play out in real time. There is another type of dialogue: indirect dialogue. It was used earlier as a possible alternative to Seth and Shannon's transactional scene; it summarized the ordering as "the server promptly took their orders." Another example is instead of using direct dialogue as shown here:

> "Hi!"
> "Hi!"
> "How are you?"
> "Good. You?"
> "I'm good."

This direct dialogue can be simply summarized:

> They greeted each other.

Other summarizing examples:

They told him that the dog hadn't gone outside
yet.
He ordered two English muffins and a carafe of
orange juice.

You can paraphrase an entire conversation:

> She ranted about how he never did things
> right, how he was always late, how he
> forgot her birthday, their anniversary, the
> lunch date at Finnegan's where he was
> supposed to meet her parents for the first
> time, and now her parents didn't like him.
> And when she had run out of breath, he
> took his turn and raged until they were
> both crying on opposite sides of the room.

An excerpt from the 2018 novel *Silver Girl* by Leslie
Pietrzyk, published by Unnamed Press, shows how to
skillfully mix indirect and direct dialogue:

> Jess would pose questions, and
> we'd wrestle out answers and laugh and
> then drop into dead-serious whispers,
> then laugh again, because everything felt
> hilarious or dead serious. My breath
> scraped my throat when I thought about
> the two of us talking across entire nights
> like it was something so normal, until
> finally I had to ask, desperate to sound
> casual, "Why do you even talk to me?" but
> the sentence burbled out on a wave of
> neediness and stupidity, and I crushed a
> pillow over my face.

First, Pietryzk doesn't show us in dialogue what the exact
questions or answers are—those are not important to the
reader's understanding of the story. What is important is
the nature of the friends' conversation and how that

reflects the friendship's dynamics: Jess poses the questions because she is the leader in the relationship; the narrator is the follower. The dramatic swing from either super serious to super silly is a microcosm of the overall volatility of their friendship. To keep the prose from becoming too much "telling," Pietryzk then shows us a specific moment, the action of the narrator's breathing and a bit of dialogue that is significant to the story. In other words, Pietryzk cuts out the unnecessary dialogue and shows only the heart of the conversation, which is the narrator wondering why Jess likes her, a major question asked throughout the entire novel. The importance of this dialogue is emphasized by being sandwiched between a little description of what the narrator intended the tone to be ("casual") and what the tone ended up sounding like ("neediness and stupidity"). Then we get a little physical action (crushing the pillow) to keep the scene from getting too heavy on the exposition and interiority.

There is an art to balancing all the different aspects of dialogue: making it sound realistic without being tediously realistic, avoiding unnatural exposition, knowing when to summarize conversation instead of showing it word for word, mixing in a little action and some internal thoughts and description so that the scene doesn't read like a screenplay. How you balance these aspects of dialogue can speed up or slow down the pacing of your story, emphasize or de-emphasize points being made, and further develop your characters.

The Mechanics and Punctuation of Dialogue

There are certain conventions with punctuating and formatting dialogue that readers have come to expect and will make for a smoother reading experience. You want the reader to focus on your story, your characters, and what your characters are saying, rather than having them puzzle out whether a character is speaking aloud or internally, or who is even speaking. So, we're going to start with the basics and then move into the not-so-basics.

In most dialogue, characters take turns speaking. Each time there is a change in who is speaking, you begin a new paragraph:

> "Feel my fingers," she said.
> "Wow, they're like icicles," he said.

Pay close attention to the placement of the punctuation marks and capitalization. The most popular format is the character's spoken word coming before the dialogue tag:

> "I like watermelon," she said.
> "I like watermelon!" she said.
> "I like watermelon?" she said.
> "I like watermelon . . ." she said.

The quoted sentence (the words that your character is saying, including the comma/exclamation point/question mark/ellipses) is enclosed between quotation marks. The dialogue tag (in this case, *she said*) is outside of the quotation marks. Notice the word *she* is lowercased. You are not starting a new sentence, so *she* is not capitalized.

You can also invert *she said* to *said she*, but in contemporary times, this inversion gives your writing an old-timey feel. See the following two examples—which sounds more appropriate?

> "I like watermelon," said she.

> "She hath curried thy favour with
> her honeyed tongue!" said I.

The answer, I hope you would agree, is the second. Exceptions to this rule would be something like:

> "But I like old-timey," said the
> pretty, blue-eyed girl.
> "Me too," said the boy in the back
> row.

It gets clunky if we were to reverse it to "the pretty, blue-eyed girl said" or "the boy in the back row said" because the tag *said* gets too far from the quoted sentence. Another way to get around this is to place the dialogue tag before the character's spoken word:

> The boy in the back row said, "The view
> from here sucks."

Notice that a comma follows the dialogue tag and the first word of the quoted sentence is capitalized. Since we're moving tags around, you can also move it to the middle:

> "I dare you," she said, "to prove
> there is a better fruit than watermelon."

If the dialogue tag interrupts the middle of a complete sentence, a comma follows the dialogue tag *said*, and the sentence continues. Notice the word *to* is lowercased because that is how it would be if the sentence was uninterrupted. If the dialogue tag is placed *in between* complete sentences, then a period follows the dialogue tag and the word beginning the next sentence is capitalized:

> "I also like a lot of other fruits,"

she said. "Want me to list them all?"

If what your character is saying is short, it doesn't really matter where the dialogue tag falls—before, after, or middle. However, if your character has a lot to say, consider placing the tag near the beginning so that the reader knows sooner rather than later who is speaking. And if your character is recounting a long, uninterrupted tale that requires more than one paragraph, begin each new paragraph with an opening quotation mark, but only end the *last* paragraph with a closing quotation mark:

> "I'm talking," she said, "for a very long time. Sentences upon sentences upon sentences upon sentences upon sentences upon sentences upon sentences upon sentences upon sentences. There is no closing quotation mark at the end of this paragraph.
> "I'm still talking without interruption. Sentences upon sentences upon sentences upon sentences upon sentences upon sentences upon sentences upon sentences upon sentences upon sentences upon sentences upon sentences upon sentences. There is no closing quotation mark at the end of this paragraph.
> "This is my last paragraph of talking. Sentences upon sentences upon sentences upon sentences upon sentences upon sentences upon sentences upon sentences upon sentences upon sentences upon sentences. There is finally a closing quotation mark at the end of this sentence!"

Punctuation marks can also quickly, and more efficiently,

indicate to the reader how your character is speaking. Question marks and exclamation marks are self-explanatory, but try to avoid using them together in ?! or repeating them in !!! or ?? etc. Using them in these ways could be interpreted as the text itself as not strong enough to convey the character's urgency. The same reasoning goes for avoiding all caps to show a character yelling. You can have *yelled* as the dialogue tag. You can use an exclamation point to indicate the yelling. You can use italics if your intention is not necessarily yelling the word but emphasizing it. In other words, strengthen the dialogue and its context so that extra punctuation mark(s) and all caps are not needed:

> Her eyes grew wide and her voice high-pitched. "What do you mean he ruined the rug?"

Other punctuation situations to be careful of: ellipses and em dashes are sometimes confused with each other. Ellipses show the speaker trailing off:

> "But I like fruit . . ." she said.

There is no need to spell out *she said, trailing off* or *she trailed off*, because the ellipses themselves already show the reader that the speaker's voice is trailing off. Ellipses can also indicate faltering or fragmented speech, hesitation:

> She said, "I know . . . I just . . ."

On the other hand, the em dash is used to indicate an interruption mid-sentence:

> "I like—"
> "Yeah, yeah," he said, "but what
> about pineapples?"

Sometimes mid-word:

> "I like watermel—"
> "Yeah, yeah," he said, "but what
> about pineapples?"

Or the speaker interrupts themself mid-thought:

> "I like—I love watermelons."

If the interrupted sentence is followed by a second character chiming in, the second character's dialogue does *not* use an em dash. As with ellipses and the trailing off example, notice how there is no need to write *he interrupted* or something similar because the em dash already shows the interruption. Also notice that there is no em dash before *Yeah, yeah*. The em dash represents the first speaker being cut off, not the interrupting person. However:

> David ran downstairs to join his parents
> already eating breakfast in the kitchen.
> "—need to stop buying
> watermelons," his dad was saying.
> "But it's his favorite fruit."

Here, the em dash shows that David, the listener, came in the middle of his dad speaking. Another way to use the em dash is to indicate a quick action that happens during the middle of a quoted sentence:

> "I think maybe"—his voice
> lowered—"you're done talking about

fruit."

This indicates that his voice lowered after saying the word *maybe*. Also notice the em dash is *outside* of the quotation marks.

Speaking of quotation marks, double quotation marks are most commonly used to indicate speaking because it is easiest to read and allows for the most flexibility. Alternatives to double quotes include em dashes, single quotes, and no marks at all. Em dashes read like scripts without the benefit of the speakers' names:

> —James Joyce loves to use this format.
> —Really?
> —Really.

James Joyce made it work, but generally speaking, it makes it difficult to keep track of who is speaking. It also makes interruptions in your dialogue look awkward:

> —I like watermel—

In the same vein, single quotation marks look awkward when there is a contraction in the dialogue:

> 'I can't stand single quotes,' he said.

The apostrophe in *can't* looks like it is the closing quotation mark.

As for dialogue without any marks, it can be done *if* done well. Cormac McCarthy is a great example of someone who can write with such clarity that the reader has no problem distinguishing dialogue from the rest of the text. While I have made up most of my own examples of dialogue, I will not attempt to make one up here. Instead, enjoy an excerpt from Cormac McCarthy's Pulitzer Prize-winning novel, *The Road* (2006), published by Vintage:

> I don't care, the boy said, sobbing. I don't care.
> The man stopped. He stopped and squatted and held him. I'm sorry, he said.

First of all, it helps that this story is written in third person. It would be much more challenging in first person because of all the additional "I" statements that would not be dialogue. He still uses dialogue tags and starts a new paragraph every time there is a change in speaker. He does make it look deceptively easy, but here is how a less skilled writer (me) might encounter problems:

> She hurried to the frowning man. Where have you been? he said. I tried to follow your directions, she said. It was all very confusing. She had wandered the park for over an hour.

Assume this is a close third on the woman's point of view. Is the sentence *It was all very confusing* spoken out loud or her internal thought? It could be argued either way, which is why I use double quotations in my own writing. If you do insist on not using quotation marks, make sure to have excellent beta readers and editors to look out for ambiguous sentences that could confuse and annoy your reader.

In contrast, the treatment of unspoken dialogue,

your character's thoughts, is less established. You can put thoughts in quotation marks just like spoken dialogue:

> "I need those leggings," she thought.

The problem with putting thoughts in quotes is that readers might see the quotes and reflexively interpret the dialogue as spoken aloud unless they're really paying attention and don't skim over the tag *thought*. The more popular alternatives are to either put the thoughts in italics or roman:

> *I need those leggings*, she thought.

> I need those leggings, she thought.

The capitalization rules remain the same; there are just no quotation marks. Because of the italics, you probably don't even need the tag *she thought*.

> *I need those leggings.* So, she bought them online with overnight shipping.

Be careful in deciding whether to use italics when you're narrating in first-person point of view. If you're already in the character's head, *all* of the narration is technically thought:

> I need those leggings. So, I buy them online with overnight shipping.

Notice how the above example is in present tense. If you're narrating in past tense, the italics could distinguish the present-tense thought from the past-tense narration:

>   *I need those leggings.* So, I bought
> them online with overnight shipping.

However, you could still get away with using all roman:

>   I need those leggings. So, I bought
> them online with overnight shipping.

Or, you could change the thought to past tense:

>   I needed those leggings. So, I
> bought them online with overnight
> shipping.

The key is to be consistent with whatever you decide, whether it's quotation marks, italics, or roman.

Like with unspoken dialogue, there is some flexibility on how to format text messages and online messaging. You can use the same formatting as dialogue but with tags such as *she texted* or *she messaged*. Or some combination of font and margins different from the rest of the text. Or use italics. Whatever you do, be consistent!

Another area that has flexibility is the treatment of numerals. Spell them out when possible. If you want some guidance from a style guide, *The Chicago Manual of Style* (2017 ed.) says, "In nontechnical contexts, Chicago advises spelling out whole numbers from zero through one hundred and certain round multiples of those numbers."

>   "I don't have sixty-five dollars. I
> don't even have a penny!"

>   "There were 101 dachshunds and
> only one chihuahua."

> "About fifty thousand people
> lived in treehouses."

Exceptions are typically made for years, trade names, or when large numbers just become unwieldly:

> "My boyfriend was born in 1982."

> "You can get a free Slurpee today
> at 7-Eleven!"

> "My number's 123-4567. Text
> me."

Again, be consistent with whatever you decide.

Generally speaking, think of whatever you put in your dialogue as being pronounced literally by your character. For example, spell out abbreviations, because people don't say *etc.*, they say *etcetera*. Don't use symbols like &, because it could look like your character is saying *ampersand* instead of *and*, or vice versa. In the same vein, parentheses are confusing because it's not clear whether the information in parentheses is you, the author, addressing the reader, or the character speaking an aside.

SAID AND OTHER DIALOGUE TAGS

The word *said* is the best all-around tag. It can be used for questions, statements, exclamations—all of it. If you worry about using *said* too many times, let me dispel you of that notion. You can't use it too many times, because it's quite the opposite; *said* "disappears" for the reader. It discreetly does its job of letting the reader know who's speaking without drawing too much attention to itself.

That's not to say you can't judiciously use

alternatives such as *asked, replied, explained, continued, added,* and *answered.* Certain genres, such as romance, tolerate more variety, while "literary" tends to use mostly *said* and *asked.*

In some cases, you may want to use more specific, descriptive tags such as *shouted, yelled, whispered, murmured,* and *snapped.* But, generally speaking (pun intended), stick to *said* unless the tag really contributes something that context and the dialogue itself cannot provide for the reader. Conversely, if you are heavily relying on tags to provide context and tone, consider strengthening your context and dialogue.

Compare these two versions while keeping in mind how you hear the characters' speaking tones. With *said*:

"I brought my pet griffin," she said, tying on her apron. "He's in the walk-in."

"Are you out of your mind?" he said. "Chef is going to be pissed."

"Griffy gets lonely," she said.

"That's unsanitary!" he said.

"Keep your voice down," she said. "You'll wake Griffy."

With each dialogue tag being different:

"I brought my pet griffin," she declared, tying on her apron. "He's in the walk-in."

"Are you out of your mind?" he snapped. "Chef is going to be pissed."

"Griffy gets lonely," she explained.

> "That's unsanitary!" he
> exclaimed.
> "Keep your voice down," she
> demanded. "You'll wake Griffy."

These tags do not add any new information for the reader, and too much tag variety can be distracting, which, in turn, can sound amateurish. Additionally, the exclamation mark in "That's unsanitary!" renders *exclaimed* redundant.

Non-*said* tags are best used when the context and the dialogue itself is not enough to show that your characters are shouting, yelling, etc:

> A server came up and whispered, "There's a griffin getting into the sauce, Chef."

The server could've spoken in a normal conversational voice or a panicked shout. The whisper shows that the server didn't want everyone to overhear and start a panic.

The following types of tags do not make sense: Tags such as *laughed, giggled,* and *sighed* are their own sounds separate from spoken words. You cannot laugh a word; a laugh is something like "ha-ha." Tags such as *smiled, glowered,* and *grinned* are facial expressions. They do not make sounds at all. Neither do tags such as *shrugged* and *nodded*. We do not grin a word; we say it, though we can be grinning while we're saying it. Alternative wordings:

> "I love your griffin." He grinned.

> "I love your griffin," he said, and sighed.

> "I love your griffin," he said with

a smile.

"I love your griffin," he said, laughing.

The first two examples are sequential. He spoke first, and then he did an action (grin, sigh). The last two examples are simultaneous, or in the case of the very last one, the laughter is interspersed with his words. Or use a nonverbal response:

He nodded, then walked away.

Dialogue tags are not always needed to indicate who is speaking. You can show who is speaking without dialogue tags by grouping a character's dialogue with an action they do in the same paragraph:

"This chicken mole is delicious," I said.
Leslie beamed. "Glad you like it!"

Here, there is no dialogue tag for Leslie, but her beaming action is paired with "Glad you liked it!" on the same line, which implies that she is the one speaking. Another way:

Leslie gave me a bowl of her chicken mole made from her grandmother's recipe.
"This is delicious," I said.
"Glad you like it!"

Here, there is no dialogue tag or action paired with the "Glad you liked it!" However, the context establishes that Leslie made the chicken mole, there are only two people in the scene, and "I" spoke first, so that means Leslie has to be the other one speaking. Once you've established who spoke first, you can continue the back and forth like this:

> "This is delicious," I said.
> "Glad you liked it!"
> "Is there any more?"
> "I froze the rest for later."

However, it is always nice to remind the reader once every few lines who is speaking:

> "You may have frozen it too soon." I was already halfway through my bowl.
> Leslie laughed. "Save room for the dulce de leche."
> "You made dessert? Marry me. Now."

Going back to the Griffy conversation, if using *said* seems too monotonous, you can incorporate all the options just shown to add variety:

> "I brought my pet griffin," she said, tying on her apron. "He's in the walk-in."
> "Are you out of your mind?" he said. "Chef is going to be pissed."
> She pouted. "Griffy gets lonely."
> "That's unsanitary!"
> "Keep your voice down," she said. "You'll wake Griffy."

Final Thoughts

All rules can be broken if done right. So, if you choose to break from convention, how do you know if you're doing it right? It is extremely difficult to read your own work objectively, to separate your intention from what actually comes through on the page. Enlist trusted editors and beta readers to see if they can understand your intent or if they get confused. Know the rules and then break the rules with intention. In other words, be clear why you are breaking from convention. Is the reason to help you achieve something that following the rules would have prevented you from doing? And is it worth the risk of confusing and turning off your reader from finishing your story? Just remember that the basic requirement of any dialogue is to clearly indicate who is saying what. To elevate your dialogue is to choose wording and punctuation that reflects your story's pacing, subtext, and character and plot development.

ABOUT CHIH WANG

Chih Wang graduated from the University of California, Riverside in Palm Desert with a Master's Degree of Fine Arts in Creative Writing. She also holds a certificate in Copyediting from the University of California, San Diego Extension. She served as fiction editor and copyeditor at *The Coachella Review* and currently copyedits for *Kelp Journal*. She runs her own freelance copyediting business, CYW Editing, specializing in fiction. A San Diego native, she spends her free time working on her novel, a contemporary fantasy, or in the air, practicing aerial silks and hammock. www.cywediting.com

References

Hill, Joe. 2017. *The Fireman*. New York: William Morrow, an Imprint of HarperCollinsPublishers.

McCarthy, Cormac. 2006. *The Road*. New York: Alfred A. Knopf, 2020.

Moreno-Garcia, Silvia. 2020. *Mexican Gothic.* New York: Del
Rey.

Pietrzyk, Leslie. 2018. *Silver Girl: A Novel.* Los Angeles: The
Unnamed Press.

WRITING BELIEVABLE CHARACTERS

Vulnerability on and off the Page

by Leslie Gonzalez

Character drives story. When reading a book or watching a film or television show, the audience is immediately introduced to the characters. While character is only one element that makes up a great story, most writers may agree that without character there would be no story.

Characters have the responsibility to connect with their audience on an emotional level. When written well, characters become three-dimensional human beings who help the audience explore and reflect the truth of human nature or the moral of the story. Characters are the reason why we weep, feel joy, or grieve in a story. It is the character's job to trigger what storytelling does best: to honor and empathize with something greater than the self. Characters—when done right—honor the struggle of what it means to be human.

This essay's purpose is not to produce a formula

for the perfect character. Instead, it works to reflect on what purpose the character operates as a three-dimensional individual who possesses empathy, vulnerability, and connection with the audience. David Corbett perfectly states in his 2013 book, *The Art of Character: Creating Memorable Characters for Fiction, Film, and TV*, that a writer's character are not cogs to the writer's narrative, but instead enrich the narrative. The writer must enrich their characters, and they do so by focusing on the internal, emotional, and softer components such as empathy, vulnerability, and the connections—as mentioned before—that make up who the characters are.

To write believable characters, the writer must accept that the emotions belonging to the characters are not separate from their own. The writer must dig deep and reflect on the self. They must be prepared to be vulnerable on the page in order to create authentic characters.

What does the writer's vulnerability have to do with building believable characters? Everything. For writers, writing is the epitome of bearing the soft flesh of the writer's belly. As shame researcher Brené Brown says in her 2011 TED Talk, innovation, creativity, and change comes from vulnerability, and to write something that hasn't been read or written before, and then eventually showing it to a public audience, is the definition of vulnerability.

Taking Brown's words into consideration, vulnerability is where believable characters are born. Nothing engages a reader more than a character who is vulnerable and wounded. A wounded character, physically or emotionally, evokes compassion, empathy, and creates a connection between the character and the reader. Having a vulnerable character is not the same as writing a weak character. Writing vulnerable characters makes them sympathetic and gives them the chance to change and become stronger, and evidently overcome the hurdles that keeps them from their goal.

PART ONE: DRAFTING CHARACTERS

FIRST DRAFT CHARACTERS: THE INITIAL SKETCH

Creating characters can be one of the most intimidating processes in storytelling. Where does the writer begin? The process varies. It can begin with a physical image, a gesture, or—such as in award-winning author Neil Gaiman's case—a voice. Writers may collect a composite of these elements from real-life examples, examples inspired by relatives or interesting friends who have memorable quirks or tastes. All of the above is a valid way to construct character. Let the writer be assured that there is no wrong way to Frankenstein a character together. There are, however, some key factors to weigh in once an idea starts to take physical shape.

Lajos Egri states in *The Art of Dramatic Writing* (1972) that in order to build characters, the writer has to think of them as three-dimensional individuals, ones where the writer should fully understand their psychology, physiology, and sociology. By acknowledging the internal and externals of character, the writer begins to understand what it means to create a three-dimensional being. They write humanity instead of imitating it, much like a puppet or an A.I. The writer needs to understand how a character thinks, how they look, and what makes up their environment, may it be the setting, their home life, their family, or their friends. Egri's formula, although thorough and beneficial, should be taken with a grain of salt. Would it be helpful to know what the character looks like? Sure. Would it be great if the writer knew what their character's vices, virtues, and childhood were like? Why not? Is it important for the reader to know? Absolutely not. Detailed descriptions of your character are not needed unless the information is necessary to drive the story forward.

Knowing a character's psychology, physiology, and sociology is only important if it matters to the story. For instance, let's say the author writes a story about an overweight teenager, how does that teenager see themself? Are they insecure about their image because of the circumstances of their environment? Have their classmates or family members harassed them? If so, how would that character's faltering self-esteem make them maneuver and visualize the world around them? How does their appearance affect the trajectory of the story? Do the circumstances of their appearance cause them to fall into self-destructive behaviors that will eventually lead to the central conflict of the story? The character's appearance, beliefs, and how they see themselves are helpful if it progresses the story. The best way to confirm its importance is to ask whether those details are worth revealing.

Take Them Out for a Test Drive

Let's say the writer has a good idea about who their character is, and that the writer is confident enough to insert their character into their story, but the writer is unsure how to animate them. This is a good time for the writer to test drive their character as a proverbial crash test dummy for—as Jack Hart references in his book *Storycraft: The Complete Guide to Writing Narrative*

Nonfiction (2015)–the "vehicle" of the narrative. The best way to test them is through scene.

The best scenes to flesh out characters are when they are faced with a dilemma. The scenes don't need to be a part of the writer's plot. To anyone else who isn't holding the pen, the scene doesn't need to exist. Indulge. The scene can be anything from what the character would do if they were confronted by a mugger, found a lost wallet, or how they would address a lost child. The point of fleshing out their actions and reactions is to better understand how they see the situation and confront their own contradictions before witnessing that action.

By exercising their fictitious limbs, the writer can easily understand how their characters externalizes their emotions, their values, and their ideas; the character's life becomes more concrete in the narrative.

A word of caution: exposition, when excessive and overdone, kills character. Exposition is telling, not showing. Yes, writers have heard the adage "show don't tell" to the point where any writer, new or experienced, just wants to bash their heads against the wall. But there is some truth to the saying. This is because it slows down the story's pace and stunts the scene's objective, which is, again, getting the character closer to the action. Think of exposition as the story's speed bump or a school zone with a twenty-five-mile-per-hour speed limit.

If the writer still struggles with how their characters hypothetically react and drive themselves, then the writer can imagine the character as an extension of themselves. By accepting the character as an extension of self, the writer is that much closer to creating a believable character and understanding the importance of connecting with their viewer on the page or on the screen.

Once the writer has a grasp of who their characters are, the next step is to begin digging into the core of that character's desires, which leads the writer to ask the most important question for any, if not all, characters in their story: "what does my character want?"

A Streetcar Named Desire, Dreams, Ambitions and Goals

Television producer Bill Rabkin once told a table of young and inexperienced scriptwriters that the most vital question to ask when writing a character is what does your character want and how do(n't) they get it? Because once the writer knows what their character wants and acknowledges their inner most dreams and desires, the drama is born.

Any characters' desire, especially the protagonist's desire, should be definitive, singular, and borderline obsessive. Egri writes, "'A pivotal character must not merely desire something. He must want it so badly that he will destroy or be destroyed . . . to attain his goal." (1972) What is at stake for the character when they pursue their desires? How important is that desire to them? When answering these preliminary questions, the writer can better understand how their character will progress. Because, let's face it, the higher the stakes, the greater the drama, therefore the better the impact.

Characters having desire is what breathes a narrative to life, but what if their wants change? What if what they want isn't what they want at all?

The Dream is *Not* the Goal

It's not so much that the writer should ask what

the character wants and how they can get it. That's only part of the equation. To create strong believable characters, the writer must allow their character's dreams to change.

Ben Loory once explained during a lecture at a low-residency program for University of California, Riverside in 2017, how a character's dreams don't need to align with their ultimate goal. It's best to have an outer objective, or the true focus on what the story is really about. That outer objective will encompass the character, merging them and their desires in the story. Loory used *Star Wars* as a perfect example about how a character's goals change and alter to fit the overall story objective.

Zoom in to Luke Skywalker. Luke didn't begin his journey wanting to become a Jedi, instead he was a farmer who wanted to go to the academy and become a pilot. That all changed after meeting Obi-Wan. After some reluctance on Luke's part, along with the death of his aunt and uncle, Luke's desires changed. While he was reluctant, all his choices still led him to be a part of the Resistance, and he ultimately became a Jedi Knight who aided in destroying the Death Star and guiding him to the true focus of the story which was to ultimately abolish the Empire. (Lucas 1977)

If Luke's desire remained the same from beginning to end, there would be no *Star Wars*. The Death Star wouldn't have been obliterated, and the Resistance would have surely been crushed.

If the writer doesn't know what their characters want, they should explore what they *think* their characters want and go from there. Even if it's as simple as being king of their local bowling alley or earning approval from their mentor or father figure. Everyone wants *something*.

PART TWO: CLARIFYING DIALOGUE AND GESTURES

ACTION AND DIALOGUE ARE YOUR FRIENDS

It's hard not to fall into the pit traps of exposition by telling the audience how the character moves through the story instead of showing them. But action is not exposition. Action can be told *or* shown, but told action is exposition and shown actions is storytelling.

So, how does a writer know if they are showing or telling? Are you listing what's happening? Or are you emersing the reader in what is happening? Slow down the action when needed and assess the situation. Even trains must slow down when arriving at their station. So, slow down enough when approaching conflict or drama, but don't stop unless it's a drop-off point. Mind the gaps and keep moving. Although it is important to show the quality of a realistic character through action, never forget the importance of dialogue. Action reveals a character by doing, whereas dialogue reveals character by voice. You need both to execute a credible or believable character.

ACTION INTERIM: MIME WHAT YOU KNOW

Gestures and mannerisms can help the writer understand character by filling in the spaces outside of dialogue. However, this is where some writers can easily fall into clichés and trite themes that make their characters sound cringy. The best way to avoid those pit traps is for the writer to ask whether their character's mannerism or gesture is necessary for the scene or if it's just to fill in space. If it is a necessary gesture to further enhance, establish a character or set the mood or tone, keep it, if it's just to fill in the space for the sake of filling it in, or to make the dialogue more interesting, chuck it. Whether it's lighting a cigarette or making constant eye contact, the writer must remind themselves that whatever their character does, they do so because it enhances their credibility as a three-dimensional individual, and not because they need to fill the scene.

The mannerisms of a character can also betray a character's thoughts and emotions. Their movement is a tool to either confirm or contradict their character's thoughts and emotional conflict. If they say one thing, but their body or reaction says another, how is that character seen by the audience? How does it make the audience understand who that character is?

Dialogue is Not the Same as Table Talk

Let's briefly dive into dialogue. As stated previously, the dialogue reveals character through voice. We're not trying to fill the spaces of our stories by meaningless chatter, instead what the writer must do is tell the reader through voice what they need to understand, what they need to get out of the things communicated between character A and character B. Does character A have an argument with character B because it will evidently lead character A to the crux of the story? Does it give the reader information that they didn't know prior? What characters say and why they say it is a push and pull of information and can add subtext to the story.

In dialogue, characters are constantly taking, giving, or asserting power. With that said, it's important to know that the power of dialogue can create subtext. It gives hints to the reader where the scene of the story is going. A good example? *Silence of the Lambs* (1988) by

Thomas Harris.

When Clarice Starling visits Dr. Hannibal Lecter in Baltimore Hospital, their exchanges are not polite prattle. There's a goal and intent in their conversation. Starling wants to know the identity of Buffalo Bill; Lecter gives her hints and clues about who Buffalo Bill is. Every time Lecter tells Starling how to find Buffalo Bill, he's not filling the space—every word enhances Lecter's character, feeds the viewer information about him, and, at the same time, provides subtext vital for the entire story, not just the case Clarice is solving.

Dialogue is also a form of action. It has the power to reveal personality, habits, speech impediments, and accents, which can tell the reader who the characters are in a way where exposition fails to deliver. As Janet Burroway says in her 2019 book, *Writing Fiction: A Guide to Narrative Writing*, dialogue has the responsibility to characterize and provide purpose in a scene. It is meant to place the reader in the present and provide exposition, scene, action, foreshadow or reminders.

There are various ways of writing realistic dialogue. But what's important to understand is that how language is spoken and read are two different creatures and should be treated as such. If the writer tries to write dialogue exactly as spoken, it will sound jarring, repetitious, and forced. To tackle dialogue in a manner that is efficient, effortless, and realistic, the writer must know the goal of that conversation. They must ask, "So, what? What is the point?"

When writing dialogue, it's acceptable to use verbal communication as a loose reference. Some of those references, as an example, would be listening to speech pattern, pauses, or tone. Burroway suggests that the next time there is a conversation, notice how the speaker may pause, dodge answers, shift the subject, interrupt, or fall silent. When noticing the speaker's behaviors, lean in. Notice, when speaking about a specific topic, how the opposite party hands over information. Do they do so easily or is there a pull back? Does their conversation evoke emotion, or does it carry vulnerability? It's not so much as what's being said, but how it's said. How much information is the writer willing to give and what does that information reveal about their character?

Conversation helps trigger change. It persuades and alters perception; it has the potential to alter a character's desire. As Burroway puts it, "The significant characters of fiction must be capable both of causing an action and of being changed by it." (2019) And since a character's desire has the opportunity to change, so does the character. Enter the character arc, or as Brown calls it, the birthplace of vulnerability. (2011)

PART THREE: EVOKING CREDIBILITY THROUGH VULNERABILITY

VULNERABILITY IS THE BIRTHPLACE OF INNOVATION, CREATIVITY, AND BELIEVABLE CHARACTERS

Let's talk about character transformation or, more formally, the character arc. A character's desires cannot change without the character experiencing change themselves. Whether it's through a dramatic transformation or steady growth, somewhere down the line, characters must change in the narrative.

Even if the character doesn't want to change, conflict should still find them. Change is essential and inevitable. That's the reality of storytelling. Even if the character utterly refuses to chase after their desire or literally does nothing to advance the story, then (like in *Star Wars*) the story must simply come to them.

Let's take an example from the movie, *Stranger Than Fiction* (Foster 2006). Harold Crick is an IRS agent who lives a banal, gray-paper life. Harold counts his brush strokes while brushing his teeth, counts the number of steps it takes from his apartment to the nearest bus stop, and imagines the sound of ocean waves when filing paperwork. Harold has no desires or ambitions outside his complacent lifestyle. That is, until he realizes that his life is literally being narrated and written by an author who foretells his death.

Trying to understand the circumstances of his life, Harold speaks to an English professor who helps him confirm whether he is the main character of someone's book or just insane. To test the theory, the professor asks Harold to quarantine himself in his apartment and do nothing—no brushing his teeth, getting the mail, or picking up the phone. By doing so, they'll determine whether he is a character in a story. If his life remains stagnant, then it would end the narrative. But if the story finds him and forces events upon him, then that confirms Harold's status as a character. Sure enough, secluded in his apartment, Harold literally does nothing until the story crashes into his apartment building via a bulldozer. The crash solidified Harold's understanding that he is, in fact, the main character of a story and is forced to move forward.

Yes to Change

There are various ways for a character to encounter change. When change occurs to a character, they must gain the necessary confidence to overcome obstacles, achieve a level of selflessness, or address a mistake that they themselves were not willing to admit. They should be able to rise up against impossible challenges and find a solution.

When a character's growth leads to change, they dig deeper into themselves and question their purpose. Corbett writes that a character who undergoes change "will experience the emotional impact of what's happened, think through what to do, suffer an insight . . . and form a decision as to what to do next ...." (2013)

When the writer thinks of change in terms of character, we imagine it to be a momentous or dramatic event. But the truth is that change varies depending on the character and how they drive the story. As long as some change takes place, there's a better chance for characters to connect with the audience. People—*humans*—change. Readers want to see change happen to characters. This is what is meant by writing round characters. These are characters who have various dimensions and are capable of change, whereas flat characters carry few characteristics and exist only to play into that role and don't stray from it.

Change doesn't always have to revolve around the protagonist. Change can be and should be applied to secondary characters and the story's antagonist, too, as long as it doesn't distract the audience from the protagonist's goal.

How writers show that change is subjective, but there is one commonality that is crucial when showing that change, and that is revealing their weaknesses and vulnerabilities. Showing vulnerability is done not solely through the character's desire, but also through the writer's willingness to be vulnerable on the page.

Vulnerability is an essential factor, and to draw out that vulnerability, the writer must dive deep in their own experiences. Once tapped, the writer should use their own feelings as an example or as a reference for their character. Think of those experiences as a footnote. This is the part where the saying "write what you know" comes into play and the writer writes through self.

ASKING BEYOND "WRITE WHAT YOU KNOW"

"Write what you know," is the universal saying bestowed to anyone who so much as picks up a pen or stares at a blinking cursor on a computer screen. The application of "write what you know" gives the reader a much more personal and intimate reading experience. It feels organic and natural. The closer the writer sticks to the truth, the more the reader believes a character, therefore, believes the story. They believe in the truth dressed in the lie, staged in the story. However, the notion of "writing what you know" is somewhat misleading. Some writers may have the tendency to take the saying for face value and it can hinder a writer's ability to write a narrative that goes beyond their own living experiences.

When we write about characters, most of us will never know what it's like to be a Hobbit on a hero's journey tasked to drop a magical ghost ring into a demon-tyrant volcano, or what it's like being the child of a womanizing god. However, some may know what it means to be tested or challenged. Many might know what it means to be underestimated, belittled, or to be someone's second choice; people do know what it feels like to prove their worth during times of struggle. That is the kernel of truth in story, and the audience will relate with those commonalities in the characters. Character helps make the ordinary struggle and the common adversity into great epics and sagas, making audiences feel connected and less alone.

Creating believable characters is not an expenditure best done lukewarm but is raw and vulnerable and exposes what humans hate the most, which is to struggle and to fail. And yet, characters who fail and struggle make for the most interesting and relatable characters in literature and media. A way for a writer to help a character become more vulnerable and help them fail is to find a common ground that levels them to their character.

FINDING COMMON GROUND

As mentioned before, desire creates drama, which means the character's failure to achieve their desires creates greater conflict. It's the sugar on the drama cornflakes. Characters are meant to stumble and lose their momentum in the story after an inciting incident. Once your character experiences failure, what they do next is crucial.

Humans connect with each other through emotion to create an empathetic or sympathetic connection. When a character is faced with a decision, the writer shouldn't just ask, "What would this character do?" but should also ask, "What would I do?" and then ask, "would they do as I would do?" Writers must dig deep into this question by exercising the key emotion needed for that character. Would the encounter or dilemma of the scene make the character feel enraged, guilty, ashamed, frightened, joyful, or pained? If so, when was the last time the writer felt those emotions mentioned? Can those moments be applied to the character? The answer is simple: Yes. Do it.

The moment the writer applies their emotions toward their character, something utterly fantastic can happen. The writer may no longer force the character to follow along a path consciously written for them, but instead validates the character's identity as a person. Applying personal emotions helps give shape to how the characters act, think, and move through the story, and—if done successfully—the characters seem to do it on their own accord. They become organic. With that said, comparing emotional notes is not enough. Sometimes the writer will have to go somewhere where it really hurts, and that is to their own failures.

Take Off the Kid Gloves

Allowing characters to fail is essential for character growth and transformation. When discussing failure, it's not about the action of failure, but rather the emotional and internal repercussions. When a character's desires are taken, given away, or jeopardized, that failure can result in feeling shame and guilt. These emotions are not necessarily negative. Shame and guilt can act as the catalyst for a character's success and triumph. They just don't know it yet.

Failure brings out the truth of a character. It forces them to look at themselves honestly and question who or what they are. It makes them question their desires.

But what is the difference between shame and guilt and why are they essential for characters to grow? Why are they essential for the writer to visit and apply for themselves?

Brown explains shame as what makes humanity

disconnect from the world around them. When their connection with others is broken it threatens people directly. The threat of disconnection from either the world or a loved one is the very necessity for character development. Guilt is a much more internal threat. Where shame creates disconnect between the character and their world, guilt creates a disconnection from the character's self, whether it be their confidence, or their ability to continue through the story. The audience needs to see and validate the struggles of the character to make a connection, for the readers to say, "they're just like me," or, "I get it." The audience has something or someone to root for.

Well-rounded characters are going to feel, one way or the other, shame and guilt. They are going to try and ultimately fail (if they haven't done so at the beginning), and in their failure the audience will have to witness that turmoil, that moment of difficulty where the character either rises or stays in their fallen state. To have a character immune to such a moment and automatically accept their failures intellectually and maturely, is not the kind of character the audience wants to see. The audience can't relate to someone who can't internalize the complexities of their own failures. That would make them inhuman and unsympathetic. What's worse? Having a character fail before the story begins and neglecting to show that failure to the reader. Both of these ideas create a gap of disconnection and delivers disappointment.

Yet, the lesson here is not creating characters who seem weepy to the point where it would be contrived and disconcerting. The lesson here is exhibiting your characters strengths and weaknesses to show readers that the character is capable to process very real human emotions, even the most embarrassing and frightening ones. It makes the character's desires that much more significant and invites the reader to be a part of the character's successes or failures.

Repercussions from failure rooted in shame and guilt come in various forms. Here is an example: imagine the protagonist is an addict and they're core desire is to stay clean and sober, but they fail and relapse. How does that character respond to that failure? Do they fail to accept their actions and justify their relapse? Do they respond with irrational hatred for themselves or for someone else? Do they hurt someone? Do they hurt themselves? Did they disappoint someone in their failure?

For story and character, it is better to find the struggle instead of finding a solution. This is particularly true because the audience may already know the solution but don't know how the character will overcome their struggles to get there.

One of the best ways to answer the question of struggle is for the writer to ask themself at what point in their life have they ever felt ashamed or guilty about a decision they made? When was the last time they couldn't look someone in the eye because they had committed something they believed was unforgivable? When someone confronts the unpleasant stresses in their lives, they can better understand how a character handles stress. With that understanding, the writer finds a common ground with their character. Struggle makes for interesting characters.

Write that down.

The only drawback for a writer to use personal

experiences is going *too* deep. The last thing a writer wants is follow their experience as an exact reference for their character's struggle, unable to move beyond the writer's experience. Corbett suggests for the writer to allow the readers to fill in the blanks. (2013) The best option is to reveal just enough to suggest what and how the character thinks or feels and give the reader the opportunity to figure out the rest for themselves. Once a character acknowledges their failures, keep it short and keep it in tandem to the story's progression.

It's important to understand and remind writers that their character's weakness does not reflect or represent the writer. Also, the ability to write imperfect characters doesn't hinder the writer's capabilities to make strong and compelling characters. People will accept imperfection even if the character's action or reaction is utterly unforgivable. The audience will tolerate a character's behavior if it remains compelling and keeps moving. In the end, it's about the character's *desire*, not about their failures. That is the objective. Vulnerability is not weakness, it's exposing imperfection.

FINDING COMMON GROUND WITH THE ANTAGONIST: IS IT POSSIBLE?

Writing vulnerability into characters is easier when applied to the protagonist—the hero. But applying this to other characters may be trickier. Especially when it comes to the antagonist—the opponent or villain.

Antagonists serve to provoke the protagonist. Antagonists can steal, destroy, or prevent the protagonist from achieving their goals. In fact, the antagonist's desires should be as vital and important as the protagonist's desires. It's a matter of balance and duality that allows tension to build within the conflict of the story. It's the antagonist's responsibility to complement and emphasize the protagonist's achievement, triggering change for the protagonist. The antagonist's actions should also assist the protagonist to rise above the story's central conflict.

With that said, how can the writer successfully deliver a believable antagonist without turning them into a caricature cartoon villain with a curled mustache? The answer is simple, just as with the protagonist, make the villain a three-dimensional individual of their own story. There is nothing more satisfying (or terrifying) than an antagonist who is just as carnal, just as *human,* as the hero of the story. The writer also needs to find common ground with the antagonist, and dive deep into morally and ethically questionable emotions and desires. The writer should find a connection and sympathetic quality about their villains so that the antagonist's influence blankets the protagonist's journey.

Here's a food for thought: the antagonist doesn't know they're the antagonist because they believe they are the hero of their own story. As an example given in "The True Origins of 'X-Men'" a 2014 article in *Rolling Stone* magazine by Brian Hiatt, take the Marvel villain, Magneto. He is one of the main antagonists of the *X-Men* comics; however, if the audience truly dissects Magneto's true intentions, they'll see that all he wants is for mutants to live in a world unbothered by human discrimination, hatred, and bigotry. On the opposite side, protagonist Charles Xavier dreams of mutants and humans coexisting. The difference between Magneto and Charles is separated by a fine spiderweb line. They both have altruistic goals motivated to achieve peace for mutant-kind, the difference is that Magneto only cares for mutants and has little regard for humanity. He enjoys the idea of humanity suffering as mutants have suffered, and that's what makes him the antagonist.

Magneto is a great example of a well-rounded antagonist because he has a goal that is understandable. Due to his backstory as a Holocaust survivor, Magneto understands what it means to live in a world of violence and oppression. His goal coupled with the *why* makes sense, as he doesn't want humans interfering with mutants and wants mutants to be freed from societal oppression.

With that said, how does Magneto's story correlate to diving deep in the writer's experiences to create a worthy opponent for their protagonist? Just as the audience may understand why Magneto justifies his reasons to create a mutant utopia, the writer must understand their antagonist by submerging themselves into their antagonist's world and finding a cause of justification for their actions. How are they motivated? What drives them or compels them to do what they do? This applies to writing even the most malicious characters.

It's not about what's morally right and wrong in society's eyes, but rather what's right and what's wrong for that particular opponent. This pits the antagonist's desires against the protagonist's, thus inciting drama. Hart believes a protagonist is defined by the strength of the opposition they face. This is where the writer needs to dig deep and accept that the antagonist—no matter how unforgivable—share a commonality.

In his Masterclass lecture, Neil Gaiman asks his class to go into their selves as their antagonists, as the bad guy, and not be afraid to ask "what would you do? What do you say? Who are you?" (2021) Dwelling in those uncomfortable scenarios can help a writer better understand who their antagonist is and why their desires matter.

ALL TOGETHER NOW

In short, credible, believable, and authentic characters are not as fictitious as they seem. They are authentic because they are *real*. They are *complicated, complex, multi-dimensional,* and perfectly *imperfect.* That's who the audience shows up for. Brown tells us that showing up and doing the work means stumbling and getting tossed around while doing it. (2011) When a writer is ready to participate with that very scary and complex thing that makes them human, they can't do so when they believe they are immune to flaw. The truth is, the writer is going to show their most vulnerable sides because innovation and creativity, especially in the realm of storytelling, is a vulnerable space.

To create requires the writer to be vulnerable on the page, and by doing so they are taking the chance to tell a story from the perspective of a character who bears the same emotional impacts and share them with the audience. To write believable characters, the characters need to be human and possess the capability to share empathy, vulnerability in order to make a meaningful, natural, and believable connection with readers.

ABOUT LESLIE GONZALEZ

Leslie Gonzalez is a freelance writer and editor from San Diego, California. Her works of fiction are published in *Mythos* magazine and *Indie IT Press* and her editorial work is published on LOCALE, OK Whatever, and

Flaunt magazine. Her writing primarily focuses on entertainment, fiction, and commercial content creation. She earned her BA in Creative Writing from California State University, Northridge, and her MFA in Fiction from UC Riverside Low-Residency program in Palm Desert.

References

Brown, Brené. 2011. "The Power of Vulnerability." *YouTube.* Uploaded by TED, January 3, 2011, 20:49. https://www.youtube.com/watch?v=iCvmsMzlF7 o&t=3s

Burroway, Janet. 2019. *Writing Fiction: A Guide to Narrative Craft.* 10th ed., Chicago: University of Chicago Press.

Corbett, David. 2013. *The Art of Character: Creating Memorable Characters for Fiction, Film, and TV The Art of Character: Creating Memorable Characters for Fiction, Film, and TV.* New York: Penguin Publishing Group.

Egri, Lajos. 1972. *The Art of Dramatic Writing.* New York: Touchstone.

Gaiman, Neil. 2021. "Dialogue and Character." *Masterclass.* Uploaded by Masterclass, May 27, 2021. 25:14. https://www.masterclass.com/classes/neil-gaiman-teaches-the-art-of-storytelling/chapters/dialogue-and-character

Harris, Thomas. 1988. *The Silence of the Lambs.* New York: St. Martin's.

Hart, Jack. 2011. *Storycraft: The Complete Guide to Writing Narrative Nonfiction.* eBook, Chicago: University of Chicago Press.

Hiatt, Brian. 2014. "The True Origins of 'X-Men.'" *Rolling Stone*, June5, 2014. https://www.rollingstone.com/movies/movie-news/the-true-origins-of-x-men-77108/

Lucas, George, Director. 1977. *Star Wars Episode IV: A New Hope.* Twentieth Century Fox. 2 HR. 1 MIN.

THE SUSPENSE IS KILLING ME

How to Build Suspense in Any Genre

By A.E. Santana

Anticipation. Apprehension. Anxiety. Worry. These are the words a writer must keep in mind when developing suspense in their story. Whether the project is an extended series or a short story, a romantic comedy or a haunting ghost tale, suspense is a versatile literary device that keeps readers glued to the page and reading long into the night.

Suspense hinges on dramatic irony, when the readers know more than the characters do. Suspense is also an emotional reaction. The readers are *worried* or *afraid* for the characters. These two aspects make suspense different from other literary devices, such as tension or mystery. Tension is the balance between two or more opposing forces, often incited by conflict. Mystery is when the author withholds information, and the readers discover the clues alongside the characters. Suspense is the mental uncertainty caused by the knowledge given by the author.

Depending on the genre, suspense can manifest in

a variety of ways. In romance, it might be when the readers know the two main characters love each other before the characters do. In horror, it may be when the audience knows the house is haunted before the new owners do. In an adventure, it can be when the readers know that the protagonist will run into trouble before the character figures it out. Of course, these are only samples, there are a wide range of ways an author may construct a suspenseful situation.

If suspense is fueled by providing the audience information, what kind of information is that exactly? What do authors let the readers know that the characters do not? Legendary director Alfred Hitchcock has an answer to that.

Lauded as the master of suspense, Alfred Hitchcock developed a scenario to illustrate suspenseful dramatic irony, sometimes known as the "bomb under the table" analogy. Although in this example Hitchcock is discussing screenwriting and directing, how suspense feels to the audience and how it is built up expands across all storytelling forms.

In a 1970 interview with American Film Institute, Hitchcock relayed a story about four people at lunch sitting around a table when a bomb unexpectedly goes off. Although shocking, this is not suspense—it's surprise. There were certain elements missing from this scene, most notably worry, to move past surprise into suspense. Hitchcock continues his analogy by replaying the same scene only, this time, there is a bomb under the table. The audience sees it, the characters do not. "The whole emotion of the audience is totally different, because you've given them that information." (Hitchcock 1970) Now the audience will watch this lunch scene with anticipation, apprehension, and anxiety. Now they watch with worry.

So, back to the question, what kind of information does the writer need to give to the reader but keep from the characters? The answer is: Anything that makes the reader worry. Let's dive deeper into the ways of crafting worry—developing suspense.

Hitchcock's analogy gets to the core of what suspense is: give the audience information. However, there is more to successfully building suspense than the bomb example details. Whether it is through an arc or an entire plot, building suspense encompasses various elements that feed into each other. To create worry, there needs to be *characters that readers care about, conflict*, and *high stakes and rising tension.* There are also certain techniques, which work best with proper pacing, that help to layer on the worry, including *staying a step ahead of the reader, foreshadowing, and callbacks, spacing out minimal action,* and *isolating the character.* All the while, the writer must note that suspense is based on the emotional reaction of the audience; it's a feeling transferring from the page to the reader.

Another element to consider is that once the suspense is built up, how can a writer avoid letting their hard-earned suspense fizzle out at the climax? By paying attention to emotional promises made through the work, keeping those promises, and by crafting an ending that is *emotionally* and *logically satisfying.* While all these elements can be applied separately, they are best used as a support system for each other—a harmonious cycle where the author takes the opportunity to feed these elements into one another.

Worrisome Things

Worry is at the heart of suspense. To achieve successful suspense, readers must worry about the characters and the situations that they are in. Will they achieve their goals? Will something bad happen to them? Will they ever discover that horrible secret? Will they make it out alive? Without worry, there is no suspense. It's the writer's job to make the readers turn to the next page in anxious apprehension. To do this, a writer can focus on three elements that create a worry-filled situation: 1) characters that readers care about, 2) conflict, and 3) high stakes and rising tension.

Characters Readers Care About

While Hitchcock's bomb example gets right to the point, he skips over the fact that readers must care that the people having lunch will be blown to pieces. Although it is hopeful that readers care about people just because they are people, that can't always be said for fictional characters. Especially characters the readers don't know much about. So, writers must create an identifiable, well-rounded, sympathetic character for the reader to worry over. Building empathy and concern for these characters is a great way to invest the readers.

Think about your favorite characters. Would you be upset if something awful happened to them? Why? What is it about these characters that you identify with? Ideally, these characters, whether they are human or not, have positive and flawed human traits. Maybe they are courageous yet stubborn. Talented but unmotivated. Strong but scared. Whatever traits they have, the most important aspect of a relatable character is either a goal or an internal struggle.

What do the characters want? What do they care about? What are the hopes, dreams, desires, and goals of the characters? What are the consequences of the characters *not getting* their desired outcome? On the flip side, writers can also create a character that readers despise. What are the consequences of that character *getting* their desired outcome? A character that readers dislike is still a character that readers care about in some way.

Alma Katsu's 2018 historical horror novel, *The Hunger*, details the infamous trek of American pioneers in the 1800s. Later known as The Donner Party, the dreadful destiny of these pioneers is well-known by most readers interested in history and/or horror. With a few hundred years removed from the events and people, and the story having been told before, it may seem that all the suspense has been filtered out of the narrative. Yet, Katsu creates suspense by writing characters that readers care about. The audience is witness to the hopes, dreams, and desires of various members of the group, creating a bond between character and reader.

In *The Hunger*, on the night before the doomed journey, Jacob Wolfinger confesses to his wife, Doris, his involvement in a young woman's death. Although he feels guilty, there is another reason the situation is heavy on his mind. Wolfinger believes that one of the families on the journey is connected to the deceased woman, and he travels in fear of being discovered. He wants a new life for him and Doris. He wants to start over. Haven't we all wanted to start over? This is an identifiable desire, which now attributed to Wolfinger (and even Doris) gives reason for readers to care about them.

With a large cast, *The Hunger* has many examples to choose from, such as Tamsen Donner, who I personally didn't care about until I discovered her deep love for her children. As the final days of the Donner party came to an end, it was Tamsen's desire to keep her children safe that made me connect with her, giving meaning and suspense to her character's story.

In these examples, readers see the pioneers as people with struggles, dreams, fears, and hopes. By building on the characters' goals or internal struggles, Katsu's creative imagining of how The Donner Party spiraled into their notorious fates is not only horrifying but also keeps readers on the edge of their seats. Readers identify with and *feel* for the characters. Having characters that readers care about (either positively or negatively) is not negotiable. It's a must. Not only does it connect the reader to the character—person-to-person—it also develops a foundation on which to build suspense.

CONFLICT

Every story needs conflict to push the plot along, create needed tension, and to put beloved characters in jeopardy (or give hated character the upper hand). The conflict, the possibility of characters not getting their desired outcome or dealing with dangerous or risky situations, feeds into how much the audience cares. Also, without conflict it may feel as if nothing is happening in the story. Conflict is the friction, the situation that went bad, the missing sibling, the lovers' quarrel, the ghostly noises at night, the case of mistaken identity. What is going wrong for the characters? What is keeping the characters from getting their desired outcome? Answering these questions will point writers to the conflict in their story.

The conflict in *Kindred,* Octavia E. Butler's 1979 science fiction novel, is pulsating with suspense. A young Black woman, Dana, is pulled from her newlywed bliss into the antebellum American South where she becomes a slave to a distant white relative until she can find a way home. Conflict is layered into the plot: the unexplained, unexpected time travel; the power dynamics of slavery and of systematic and cultural racism; Dana's struggle with her heritage and her marriage; her battle to return home and stay home. Early on, Dana attempts to explain her situation to Rufus, her white ancestor. "This is a crazy thing that's happened to us . . .. But when you're in trouble, somehow you reach me, call me, and I come . . ." (Butler 1972, 62)

Mentioned here is one of the main conflicts, the unexplained time travel. The sharing of this information with Rufus creates confusion and more conflict for the characters, which parallels how knowing that Dana can be swept back into time at any moment creates suspense for readers.

The conflicts in *Kindred* are not only dangerous but also in direct opposition with Dana's desires, dreams, and world perspective described in the beginning of the novel. Before she was transported back in time, Dana and her husband were in the midst of moving into their new home, and Dana was excited to focus on her writing career. Her life seemed to be on track, and she began to think that she was safe and grounded. From there, she is yanked away from her safety, desires, and dreams. Her life is no longer her own and all she had before, including the vague sense of freedom, is gone.

Since the characters know Dana's hopes and desires, they can care for her, which feeds into the conflict—making the struggle an emotional and suspenseful one.

HIGH STAKES AND RISING TENSION

Part of the conflict for the characters is that they want something, and they can't have it, or are having difficulty in getting it. But as the story progresses, the stakes need to go up. Do the characters' goals change or intensify as the conflict bears down on them? How is the danger or risk growing? What is the worst thing that can happen if the character doesn't reach their goal? Double it.

Tension, as mentioned earlier, is the delicate balance between opposing forces. The characters want something but there is conflict keeping them from achieving their goals, and from this, tension is created. By creating high stakes, the tension will naturally begin to rise. At the same time, writers must ensure that the plot is moving along and that they are not hitting the same beat (the same topic, issue, circumstance, etc.) once it has been resolved. If not resolved, those elements need to increase.

Get risky, and don't be afraid to hurt your characters physically, mentally, and emotionally. These are characters that readers care about, let the readers hurt along with them. Near the climax of the story, no matter the genre, the stakes must be more intense than they were at the beginning.

The stakes start high and rise with the growing tension in *Mexican Gothic* (2020) by Silvia Moreno-Garcia. Noemí Taboada leaves her lavish life of parties behind to check on her cousin, Catalina, who recently moved to the mysterious High Place after marrying the equally mysterious Englishman, Virgil Doyle. Soon it becomes apparent that getting out of High Place is more difficult than it seems.

As Moreno-Garcia drips more information in for the reader, she also ups the stakes as Noemí's wants and desires change. This is especially seen as Noemí goes from wanting only to check on Catalina to saving her, then the need to save them both. Eventually, she has a desire to liberate Virgil's cousin, Francis.

On page 136, the reader begins to see how Noemí's budding affection for Francis will eventually lead to heightened stakes and tension: "He had an almost nonexistent upper lip, eyebrows that arched a little too much, heavy-lidded eyes. She liked him nevertheless." (Moreno-Garcia 2020) Becoming acquainted and close with Francis makes Noemí's situation worse instead of better.

For Noemí and her cousin, the stakes have been raised by feelings of compassion. Leaving High Place becomes increasingly complicated. The reader's apprehension and worry build, not only for Noemí and Catalina's ever more difficult escape, but also for Noemí and Francis' possible connection. This is suspense, as the reader is aware of something the character is not— something that will cause more trouble and tensions, raising the stakes.

PACING MAKES PERFECT

While there is no suspense without worry, being able to drag that worry out and milk it makes for effective anxiety, apprehension, and anticipation. Going back to Hitchcock's bomb analogy, the suspense can be dragged along, stirring unease in the audience. But how long does the bomb count down for? A minute? Ten minutes? How long is not enough, and how long is too long? The answer depends on a myriad of elements: length of story, amount of buildup, logical plot progression, etc. The author will need to test the waters and experiment to discover what works best in their story. Successfully paced and crafted suspense will be able to be stretched as the author needs it.

Pacing isn't just about spreading plot and action over the storyline, but also incorporates timing and delivery for maximum impact. When in the story does the suspense start? When does the suspense increase? When does it conclude? Like pacing, the author will need to experiment with timing in the story to get it right. But to help get a handle on pacing for suspense, there are a few techniques a writer might want to consider: 1) staying a step ahead of the reader, 2) foreshadowing and callbacks, 3) use less action and gore, and 4) isolate the characters.

A STEP AHEAD

For suspense, the reader must be aware of the conflict or possible conflict ahead of the characters. However, writers must not give away plot endings or thoughtful twists because then the tension in the "What will happen?" will dissipate. All the writer's hard work to create suspense will be gone. Imagine suspense as a deflated balloon. The writer blows up the balloon, creating suspense. Giving away plot twists too soon is allowing the balloon to release before reaching its maximum size.

The reader must be a step ahead of the character, and the writer must be a step ahead of the reader, promising that "things are not as they seem." So, while the reader knows the house is haunted, or the two characters are perfect for each other, the author must also hint that something more terrible or exciting is about to happen. The missing child is found but there's something off about them now. The discarded diary is also a treasure map. Whatever the twist, the idea is to lead the reader to something more. By being a step ahead of readers, the author accumulates conflict, high risks, rising tension, then thoughtfully paces these elements throughout the story.

Note: Staying a step ahead of the character is not a red herring or a trick, because it's not meant to throw readers off. Nobody likes being tricked, even in literature or film. Examples of tricking the reader are: When an author never gives any hint or never introduces the killer, thief, etc. When an author establishes rules then changes those rules (or offers contradictory information) mid-story or at the end. When an author intentionally provides information that leads nowhere and is never resolved. When an author creates a scene or situation without logically leading the reader into it because the writer wanted to "wow" or surprise the reader. This list can go on. Instead, being a step ahead gives the readers all the information they need but displays that information in such a way that the outcome is less predictable.

A haunted house story that tackles themes of generational trauma, grief, and racism, *The Good House* (2003) by Tananarive Due delivers suspense by keeping the audience well informed yet staying a strategic step ahead. After the death of her son, Angela Toussaint finds herself battling an evil spirit that has been torturing her family for decades. The reader knows that the house is haunted, knows that Angela must discover the secrets her grandmother (and son) kept, and Due masterfully keeps building the suspense as more information is dripped into the novel.

In one scene, the story of how The Good House became cursed is told from the point of view of the evil spirit as it possesses Angela's ex-husband, Tariq. Although the spirit's story does answer some questions for the reader, it is also giving this information to a possessed Tariq who is out to destroy Angela. With Tariq having more information than Angela, he holds the upper hand. How will Angela survive now? The audience will have to keep reading to find out. (Due 2003)

Here, the suspense builds because the information from the evil spirit creates more cause for worry—it grates on the conflict and rouses tension as readers realize how much danger Angela is in. Although Due has provided more information to readers in this scene, she stays a step ahead of readers by creating a situation where that information causes worry without solving the conflict. The evil spirit may be seen as an unreliable narrator, sewing discord while offering knowledge. In this instance, it may be difficult for readers to guess what will happen next. Being a step ahead is not tricking your readers or giving them information that is meant to be solved like a puzzle, rather, it is providing information that will cause worry.

Note: All information must always propel the reader forward into the next scene.

FORESHADOWING AND CALLBACKS

Foreshadowing is a technique that feeds into staying a step ahead, developing suspense by implying that the conflict will happen or worsen. This can be done in variety of ways. The reader can see something happen to another character early on that will eventually happen to the protagonist. The main character can mention a fear that will eventually come true. The impending conflict can be discussed by the narrator or other characters. How ever the writer choses to implement foreshadowing, the idea is to give a hint disguised as casual information or description. Also, the writer must ensure that there is enough time to build high stakes and raise the tension around these hints before the climax.

Note: The outcome must never come as an unwarranted surprise. A proper foreshadow makes readers go "of course!" after finally receiving the revelation, and never feel tricked (see a pattern here?).

To build on the foreshadowing, some writers use a technique known as "callback," a term borrowed from comedians. This is successfully done when something from before, like a punchline or a forewarning, is mentioned to the audience again at a moment when it is most impactful.

Callbacks can be used multiple times, but the moment delivered, and the delivery itself, is important. Don't let callbacks disappear into the action or details, and don't let the callback seem too obvious, ruining the revelation. For example, using the same phrase as a callback is a good way to jog the reader's memory of something that was hinted at before. But be sure that the wording is used in such a way that not only is it calling back to the foreshadowing but also moving the story forward. Don't get bogged down in the same beat. Foreshadowing and callbacks, peppered in as pacing allows, can help create successful and intelligently crafted suspense.

In *The Year of the Witching* (2020) by Alexis Henderson, foreshadowing is used to set the stage not only for the protagonist's revelations about the Puritan-like city of Bethel but her self-revelations too. Immannuelle has a strange attraction to the surrounding Darkwood, a shunned place where witches lurk, that she tries to ignore: " . . . the Darkwood still had a hold on her, as if it was calling her home again." (Henderson 2020, 27) This foreshadowing creates a place for suspense to fester and grow. Why does the character feel this way? What does this mean? The reader is given information, and now they can worry over it.

As Immanuelle learns more about her parents and herself, callbacks to her initial uneasy attraction to the Darkwood are used to remind the reader that something big or bad is going to happen, adding to the suspense. On page 140, Immannuelle ruminates on the knowledge of her mother being pregnant with her while staying in the Darkwood, "her first home . . .." (Henderson 2020) On page 200, a snippet of Immannuelle's mother's journal describes fleeing Bethel to make "a home in the woods" (Henderson 2020) with her unborn child.

The idea of the accursed Darkwood being home to Immanuelle is used as foreshadowing for her personal discoveries, and callbacks to this idea are placed throughout the book, building on the apprehension and anticipation.

Henderson's use of foreshadowing and callbacks are subtle and direct. Yet she does this in such a way that she is not hitting the same beat twice. Rather, she uses unresolved existing information to create suspense for the readers and to move the plot forward. The more information the reader gets, the more worrisome the situation becomes. This is the value of foreshadowing and callbacks when crafting suspense—creating a familiar term, theme, word, action, or scene to setup and remind readers to stay on guard.

USE LESS ACTION (AND VIOLENCE AND GORE)

Suspense is the anticipation of what will happen. On the page, action usually happens in real time. So, when crafting suspense into a moment or into an overall arc of a story, cutting back on the action will keep the reader in suspense, and from undercutting the climax. Think about your favorite books or movies. When does the big fight scene happen? Usually toward the end of the story, because after the end of that major confrontation where have all the tension and conflict gone? What happened to the suspense? The suspense, conflict, and tension have dissipated, liberated from the minds of the audience. So, action best comes after suspense; it acts as a release after the apprehension of waiting to see how characters interact with one another—the showdown, the attack, the confrontation. Suspense is the buildup; action is the release of it.

For those writing horror, thrillers, and other genres where action may be detailed in a more gruesome way, it's good to keep in mind that for violence and gore, less is also more for the same reason. Violence and gore are types of actions that are also shock elements. They may even be used as horrific surprises. It is also good to keep in mind that no matter how shocking violence and gore can be, readers can easily be desensitized if those elements are used too much, too often. This desensitization lessens the impact of suspense. But the reverse is also true; to bump up the suspense, lessen the violence and gore.

On the subject, Hitchcock says in a 1964 interview with Huw Wheldon that horror belongs in the mind of the audience, not on the screen (or on the page). In this instance, the term horror is being used as an element that causes shock, like violence or gore. Hitchcock continues, saying that when he was making *Psycho*, he started out with some rough and violent scenes but cut it back: "[T]here was less and less violence but the tension, in the mind of the viewer, was increased considerably." (Hitchcock 1964)

Although Hitchcock is discussing horror (violence and gore), the same is true for any major confrontation or action scene. Writers should use this to their advantage. Successful suspense builds up to the action but is not the action itself. Pace out the action, especially violence and gore (if any), to support and heighten suspense.

Antioch (2020) by Jessica Leonard is a horror, mystery thriller. As a mystery, information is purposely withheld from the audience. However, Leonard creates suspense by giving enough information that makes readers aware of something terrible happening in the background. The audience knows there's a serial killer, Vlad the Impaler, on the loose. They know that Bess is receiving strange messages on her radio. They know that someone (or thing) is targeting Bess. But a large portion of the action and, especially, the gore has already happened before the audience discovers it. At the same time, the readers know that the terrible events are not yet over.

For example, Bess discovers her house to be in

disarray after the police have sworn the serial killer has been locked up. On page 77, Leonard writes, " . . . she would take comfort in the knowledge that it wasn't Vlad. Or maybe it was." (2020) This leaves readers juxtaposed between the past attacks and the attacks to come, creating a suspense-filled limbo of apprehension without a lot of the action, violence, or gore happening in front of the readers.

It is in these spaces and moments when suspense is at its best, when the reader knows what's going on but not what's going to happen. The writer must let the anticipation, the apprehension, the anxiety—the worry— grow in the readers' minds. Lessening the action (violence and gore) will help to create these suspensefully pregnant moments in the story.

ISOLATE THE CHARACTERS

Another technique that can be used to add suspense is to isolate the character, especially if the character depends on the support of others to get them through the conflict. This technique must be carefully considered in the pacing of the story and work alongside the conflict, high stakes, and rising tension. Depending on the length of the story, isolating characters can come quickly, or several chapters in, but must happen at a time when the impact will be the biggest. To isolate a character—cutting them off from support or love or information—only to give that support back again, too soon, is a waste of time and destroys suspense.

Catherine House (2020) by Elisabeth Thomas is a moody, gothic, dark academia horror that plays with protagonist Ines' isolation throughout the plot. In the beginning of the novel, Ines self isolates. She doesn't go to class, uses partying and sex as a form of escapism instead of connection, and only befriends her studious and emotionally unavailable roommate, "Baby." As situations change, Ines also changes, looking to connect more deeply with her studies and peers. As Ines is ready to make commitments that will seemingly propel her into a positive future, she makes a series of emotional decisions that lead to her physical isolation and separation from all the relationships she had made.

In this next scene, Ines must suffer the consequences of rule breaking at Catherine House and is placed in solitary confinement. She has been here once before, but by the strange, distanced way the aide is treating her, the reader can tell that this situation is different, allowing for trepidation to creep in. "This aide only straightened, stared at me with an expression I couldn't quite read ...Then the door closed, and I was alone in the dark." (Thomas 2020, 286) Because the character had made so many meaningful connections throughout the novel—friendships, a love interest, a refocus on her studies, etc.—her physical isolation toward the end of story carries an apprehension and anxiety that her emotionless self-isolation lacked. For this reason, this isolation is overwhelming, slowly breaking Ines down, leaving readers to worry about her.

In the above example, Ines' isolation is physical that, in this case, also lent itself to emotional and mental isolation. But characters can be isolated from others who they still see and interact with. Perhaps there has been an argument, hurt feelings, or miscommunication that keeps the characters from supporting each other—and that's the point: remove all support systems. This is a good way to feed conflict and tension, building the suspense.

THE BIG PAYOFF

In his bomb under the table analogy, Hitchcock also expresses that the bomb must never go off—at least without intervention. The bomb exploding is action, is gore, is the climax. Once that bomb goes off, that's the end of the suspense, and what is the reader left with? An abrupt and unsatisfying ending.

So, how does a writer end that suspenseful moment or arc with the right payoff if the bomb can't go off without intervention? Maybe the bomb is found before the last second and is flung away. Maybe someone throws themselves over the bomb. In any case, the resolution needs to make sense without being predictable. That is the key to a suspenseful payoff. Two important factors play into landing the end of a suspenseful moment or extended arc: 1) emotional full circle and 2) logical satisfaction.

SPOILER ALERT: this section contains endings to *The Only Good Indians* by Stephen Graham Jones, *The Stand* by Stephen King, and *There There* by Tommy Orange.

EMOTIONAL FULL CIRCLE

Throughout the story, a good writer would have made emotional promises to the reader and keeps every promise at the end. The lovers reunite. The villain is destroyed. The city is saved. But this is the bomb going off without interference. A good way for a writer to intervene with the proverbial bomb is to bring the ending to an emotional full circle. The lovers are reunited after learning what it means to be a better partner. The villain is destroyed, but so is the hero's moral code. The city is saved at the cost of too many lives. Emotional promises can be sad or happy, depressing or inspiring, etc., depending on themes, style, and so on. Whatever the emotional promise is, it must be met with an ending that fulfills the story's sentiment in a reasonable and pleasing way.

In Stephen Graham Jones' *The Only Good Indians* (2020), a vengeful spirit known as Elk Head Woman stalks four men who had killed her and her unborn calf. Throughout the novel, Elk Head Woman terrorizes the men, demanding justice and retribution for their crime. The spirit kills the four men, but her thirst for vengeance is unsatisfied and she goes after Denorah, the daughter of one of the men. The novel ends with the Denorah protecting Elk Head Woman and stopping the cycle of violence.

" . . .[Denorah's] fathers have stood at the top of this slope behind a rifle, and the elk have *always* been down here, and it can stop . . ." (Jones 2020, 303) This ending keeps the emotional promises of justice and retribution, because Denorah's compassion—especially in the wake of her biological father's death—brought those sentiments full circle more so than violence could have.

If Denorah would have beaten Elk Head Woman by force, the ending would have had relief but may have also felt hollow and predictable. The violent, forceful ending is one that audiences have already seen but, on top of that, the promise of the wrong against the elk spirit being righted wouldn't have been realized. Although Elk Head Woman was the novel's antagonist, she was still a sympathetic character. Her arc needed to come full circle;

she needed an emotionally satisfying ending. Granting Elk Head Woman justice and retribution with compassion allowed for the suspense that had built up over the course of the novel to pay off big emotionally.

LOGICAL SATISFACTION

While satisfaction is fueled by emotions, as is suspense, the big payoff at the end of a suspenseful arc or book must also make sense logically. Do the action and details lead up to the climax if the reader goes back and pieces everything together? Or does the ending seem to be tacked on, or come out of nowhere? For example, the end of Stephen King's 1978 epic novel, *The Stand*, poses the "good" vs "evil" survivors against each other in a showdown in Las Vegas. While the evil survivors are thwarted by a blast from an A-bomb, and the promise of good prevailing over evil is kept, there is no suspense in that ending.

The anticipation of the opposing groups going head-to-head, and someone dealing directly with the main antagonist, Randall Flagg, were never satisfied. These two conflicts were built up over the course of the novel, but when the A-bomb went off, it took away the possibility of those major confrontations, both of which would have been logically satisfying endings. So, all emotional promises made by the novel were not kept. If concluded with a direct altercation between the opposing groups or with a final showdown with Flagg, those possibilities teased through the novel would have been satisfied. The ending to *The Stand* is the bomb going off under the table without intervention.

This does not mean that *The Stand's* ending was

poor or bad. Endings come in all shapes and sizes. But for an emotionally satisfying ending, a logical conclusion is something to keep in mind. For instance, in the 2018 novel *There There* by Tommy Orange, the story builds up to a logically satisfactory ending based on the information previously provided to readers. *There There* follows several characters with various claims to Indigenous heritage and their struggle to reconcile their identities with how they feel, how they think they should feel, and how they believe other people see them. Each story leads to the ending, where many of these characters convene at a large multi-tribe powwow that ends in disaster.

In this next example, Tony Loneman, who had hoped to dance in his tribe's traditional regalia, is shot at the powwow. He struggles through the pain, but is able to bring down the gunman, sacrificing his life. Tony feels himself slip in and out of consciousness, and his last thoughts are shared with the readers. He is four years old again and is washing dishes with his grandmother. "She keeps wiping the bubbles on the top of his head. He keeps asking her: *What are we? Grandma, what are we?* She doesn't answer." (Orange 2018, 288)

Although the novel ends in violence, destruction, and death, this a logically satisfying ending. While sad or unfair, it is also reasonable that the novel ended in this situation. The emotional themes of identity are brought full circle with Tony's flashback, and his self-sacrifice is in character for him but also a poignant tribute to the rest of the characters. Each of the stories had hit on themes of identity, violence, or death in some manner, as these themes are woven into the lineage of the characters. This makes the ending of *There There*—while devastating—

emotionally and logically satisfying, which allows the suspense to play out without blowing up with an abrupt, out-of-place action or situation.

It may be a good idea for writers to take into consideration that all stories have some suspense to them. So, for this reason, it also may be a good idea to consider emotionally and logically satisfying endings in all stories, no matter the genre or format.

In Summary

To recap, suspense is a literary device for more than mysteries or horror. Knowing how to create, build, and end suspense is useful in any genre. The techniques used to craft suspense are meant to work in harmony and feed into each other. As one element is created, it will support the next element or device: characters that readers care about, conflict, and high stakes and rising tension.

Subsequently, pacing and time deeply affect suspense and can be used to a writer's advantage by staying a step ahead of readers, using foreshadowing and callbacks, spacing out minimal action (and gore), and isolating the characters. At the end of the story, readers are looking for the big payoff. Hopefully, the writer has created a suspenseful situation that hinges on emotional themes that will be brought full circle to the delight or horror of the reader. But this ending must also make sense logically, following the plot, details, and other elements that created the suspense for an ending that is satisfactory, not a trick or an out-of-place thing.

ABOUT A.E. SANTANA

A.E. Santana is a Southern California native who grew up in a farming community surrounded by the Sonoran Desert. A lover of horror and fantasy, her works can be found in *Latinx Screams*, *Demonic Carnival III*, and other horror anthologies. She is the managing editor for Kelp Journal & Books. A.E. Santana is a member of the Horror Writers Association and has particpated in several horror panels, including "No Longer the Scream Queen: Women's Roles in Horror." She received her MFA in fiction from the University of California, Riverside's low-residency program. Her perfect day consists of a cup of black tea and her cat, Flynn Kermit. Discover more at aesantana.com. Twitter and Instagram: @foxflur

References

Butler, Octavia. 1979. *Kindred*. Boston: Beacon Press, 2003, p. 62. Kindle edition.

Due, Tananarive. 2003. *The Good House*. New York: Atria Books. Kindle edition.

Henderson, Alexis. 2020. *The Year of the Witching*. New York: Ace Books, pp. 27, 104, 200.

Jones, Stephen Graham. 2020. *Only Good Indians*. New York: Saga Press, an imprint of Simon & Schuster, p. 303.

Katsu, Alma. 2018. *The Hunger*. New York: G.P. Putnam's Sons, an imprint of Penguin Random House. Kindle edition.

King, Stephen. 1978. *The Stand: The Complete & Uncut Edition*. New York: New American Library, 1991.

Leonard, Jessica. 2020. *Antioch*. San Antonio: Perpetual Motion Machine Publishing, p. 77.

Hitchcock, Alfred. 1964. "Huw Wheldon Meets Alfred Hitchcock." Interview by Huw Weldon. *Monitor*, BBC, July 5, 1964. Video, (TIME). Accessed from *The Alfred Hitchcock Wiki*, The Hitchcock Zone, Jan. 2, 2017. the.hitchcock.zone/wiki/Monitor_(BBC,_05/Jul/1964).

Moreno-Garcia, Silvia. 2020. *Mexican Gothic*. New York: Del Rey, p. 136.

Orange, Tommy. 2018. *There There*. New York: Alfred A. Knopf, p. 288. Kindle edition.

Hitchcock, Alfred. 1970. "The Harold Lloyd Master Seminar with Alfred Hitchcock." Interview with Harold Lloyd. American Film Institute. Video, (TIME). Accessed from "The Golden Age of Hollywood." *Master Seminars from the AFI Archive*, American Film Institute. www.afi.com/master-seminars-from-the-afi-archive/.

Thomas, Elisabeth. 2020. *Catherine House: A Novel*. New York: Custom House, p. 286. Kindle edition.

THOUGHTS ON FINDING YOUR VOICE

by David M. Oslen

"When you are tyring to find your writing voice don't try to emulate any writer, not even your favorite. Sit quietly, listen, listen again, then listen some more and write out everything the voice says with no censoring —none —not one word."

~ *Jan Marquart,* The Basket Weaver

Voice is something that I obsessed over for far too long. I think the idea of "finding your voice" is problematic at its inception, because voice is innate. I studied for years at Stanford continuing studies and we read a lot of literary fiction, some with beautiful sounding prose. Fine, poetic, and purple. And there were a lot of students there who really prized their sentences, and the poetry of their language. And to be sure, there were a lot of writers with gorgeous writing. I started to obsess about how my sentences sounded. About my word use. About the prettiness and poetry of my language.

And, to be honest, I think it took me entirely in the wrong direction in learning how to write well. Good writing uses vigorous English. Good writing is clear and concise. Good writing stays out of its own way, and tells a story that breaks hearts, mends souls, and connects us to that ethereal plane of consciousness so that, for just a brief moment of our existence, we can be rid of our existential pain. Your voice is your voice. Not the voice you contrive when you're trying to sound like a writer, but the simple direct voice inside you that flows when you are really onto something big in your writing, and it just has to pour out of you with no thought given to how pretty it sounds.

I recently read *A Swim in a Pond in the Rain* by George Saunders. I don't know if the book came along at the right time in my writing life (as things tend to do), or if his guidance particularly resonated with me. But, after nearly a decade of focusing on craft and trying to find my style and my voice, I realized my voice was there the whole time. I just had to get out of my own way. I highly recommend buying and reading his book on crafting short stories.

There are two exercises that I learned that blew my world, I have seen them before in creative writing courses, but they are also present in the Saunders' book. I love them both. The first I'll share with you is probably the most important voice-based lesson I've ever learned. Voice, I have found, is often overlooked and not discussed as much as other craft elements. I think this is because voice is something that is difficult to teach. You can't say to a new writer, sound more like Hemingway. That would be insulting and weird. No, instead, we are instructed via craft elements and whether or not the story is working. This is the workshop model. This is great. But I always wondered what *my* voice was, and where to find it. Most of us start, and continue, by emulating writers we admire. This may be a good place to start, but it is not a great place to stay for too long, in my humble opinion. And for good reason. They're not you.

The first writer, post high school, that I loved was John Updike. We read a short story called "Flight" in one of my classes. His prose was so unique, and gorgeously wrought, and had such an academic yet poetic polish that it made me want not to just to write, but to write like *him*. Saunders notes in his book that he wanted to write like Hemingway. But these early influences can become problematic to your development. Though I tried, I could not even come close to writing and sounding like Updike. That is nowhere near my register. Saunders' stories (admittedly) are also not like Hemingway's. And they are still wonderful. So, how do we get these voices out of our heads?

Well, for over a decade, when I sat down to write, I put on my writing "cap." Meaning, I sat down with the intent of writing something big and important, sounding smart and poetic. The drivel that came out was awful. Every time. It didn't start to get better until I could untether myself from that process.

The exercise that brought this out in the open for me is simple and forces you to turn off your "writer" mind and think about writing simply and powerfully with as few words as possible. The muscle memory from this exercise stays with me. In fact, I think about it every time I write now. I turn off my "writer" mind and write in the simplest form I can; the results allow my own personal voice the freedom to move about on the page. The resulting work feels more "me." And I sound nothing like Hemingway, or Updike. I use this technique with all of my writing now.

Write a 450-word short story using and recycling forty-five chosen words. Keep track of the words. Remember: they can repeat themselves, but don't go over the word count.

Question upon completion: When you do this exercise, are you surprised or intrigued by the words you ended up using? Do you think understanding the connotation of your chosen words help in understanding your voice?

The second exercise that helped me find my voice is an exercise in revision. This is often taught in creative writing classes and very effective. You have to find how lean, or heavy, your voice is as a writer. You don't have to be a Gordon Lish Minimalist or have pages of dense prose. Use your editing eye, pass after pass, on your draft to revise it into your finest work. This is also part of your voice. To cut, edit, and pour over our prose dozens, if not hundreds of times. And all those micro changes, word shifts, and smoothing out of the prose changes the voice. The rest of your voice is the resulting prose after that process.

1.) Take a short story you have written, a draft, or just write something new, at least 500 words, then cut 150 words. Then cut a hundred more. Which draft is the best? Be honest with yourself. It sounds crazy, but this exercise works.

ABOUT DAVID M. OLSEN

David M. Olsen is editor and contributor to the surf-noir anthology, *The Silver Waves of Summer* (Kelp Books, August 2021). His work has appeared in *Catamaran Literary Reader, The Rumpus, The Coachella Review, Close to the Bone, Scheherazade,* and elsewhere. He attended Stanford's OWC program in novel writing and holds an MFA in Creative Writing and Writing for the Performing Arts from the University of California, Riverside in Palm Desert. David is a former fiction editor at *The Coachella Review* and is currently the editor-in-chief at *Kelp Journal*. He is at work on a collection of linked short stories, a novel, and a chapbook. He resides on California's central coast where he surfs regularly.

References

Saunders, George. 2021. *A Swim in a Pond in the Rain: In Which Four Russians Give a Master Class on Writing, Reading, and Life.* London: Bloomsbury Publishing.

Updike, John. 1959. "Flight." *The New Yorker*, August 15, 1959. https://www.newyorker.com/magazine/1959/08/22/flight-3.

LITERARY V. GENRE

A Difference in Preference

by A.M. Larks & A.E. Santana

"What do you write?" This can be a nerve-wracking question, at any point in your writing career, but especially for someone still discovering their place in the writing world. Both the authors below have struggled with this question, thinking and overthinking what to say. If you say that you write literary works, people may nod approvingly because it sounds impressive, but do they know what that means? Do you? But what if you say that you write genre work like speculative fiction? Will you be dismissed? Will you have to argue for the validity of hundreds of books and thousands of readers?

These questions and their brethren come from real-world interactions and are part of understanding your craft, and what you or others may imagine is your place in the writing world. But where do these notions come from? What is the difference between literary and genre fiction?

In this section, "literary" author A.M. Larks and "genre" author A.E. Santana separately reflected on what they thought made these labels distinct (or not so distinct). Together, their essays are an interestingly cohesive observation on audience expectation, marketing, purpose, and style.

FROM THE "LITERARY" AUTHOR:
A.M. LARKS

When I first started writing, I wasn't prepared when people started asking me the question of "what do you write?" I didn't know that the answer would be important, especially as a fiction writer, and that the conversation tone and tenor, depth, and interest, would inherently change after I answered it. I didn't really think there was a difference. I mean, certainly I knew there were genres—even genre books—and as an English Lit major I was all too eye-rollingly familiar with the literary greats and the canon. But as I came to writing later in life, I hadn't yet decided on my writer identity. That's what I was going to school for, wasn't it? Wasn't *that* (who I was as a writer) what I was going to learn? And ultimately, wasn't good writing just good writing? I never understood why it mattered, why anybody was asking.

Now, that I have had a few years in the writing world, I have developed an identity and an answer to why this topic is important: art is not created, produced, nor distributed in a vacuum. Asking "what do you write?" is the writer's version of, "what kind of dog do you have?" at the dog park. That doesn't mean that non-husky owners can't talk to the husky owners. This one simple question allows us to seek out a community of writers who like what we do. I have found out that our literary or genre identities allow us to bond with like-minded individuals. It is not meant as a measure in which to enact exclusivity, but rather as one used to find your peoples. But people are people, even when they are looking for "their peoples," and by that, I mean this question can be used to ostracize and even snub writers of one of the other identities. Prevailing book culture has the literary folks with their focus on settings, characters, and really weird literary devices separated from the genre lovers and their focus on plot, structure, and, at times, predictability. Are those who read *The New Yorker* snobbier than those who love *Strange Horizons*? Are readers of Cozies better in some way than those who are fans of J.D. Salinger? The answer is a resounding "No!" It is obviously a matter of preference as much as it is community. We all like what we like, which is why we like it, and because we like it, we think it's great, we tell people it's great, and we want to hang with others who think it's great too.

Underlying both community and personal preference are market forces. The market, while important to understand, has limited application in the art-making process. The market divides authors into categories because where you are shelved and who you are shelved with matters to readers (consumers) who want to know what they are getting and where to get what they want. Readers also want to know about other works that are like that last thing they read/liked/heard about. So, if someone likes Zora Neale Hurston, will they have a greater propensity to like your southern-based novel? But they won't, if what you have written is actually more like a western and appeals to fans of Elmore Leonard. Where you are shelved is only a concern if you have a finished piece of writing. Think final draft. I find it premature for writers to be resolute about a work in progress. If it is unfinished, it is subject to change and therefore you as are writer are subject to change with it.

Thinking of your intended audience is a good consideration in the editing stage of drafting, however. Readers come to certain books with their own expectations based on the above marketing. A pizza without a crust and sauce is just melted cheese and toppings. Still insisting on calling that dish a pizza fails to respect what the general purchasing public understands is pizza. Making sure that you have delivered on your fast-paced plot or your metaphor-laden hero's journey is tantamount to staying in business as a pizza place. As an artist you can make your cheesy, gooey mess and we will still buy it, but let's make sure that we call it as cheesy gooey mess and not pizza.

This journey and the answers to these questions are inherently personal. For me, knowing that I am a literary writer has its advantages. I know that my readers expect a certain number of literary devices in my work. I know who my people are, what magazines to submit to, what conferences to attend. I know who my work might compare to, where it would be shelved in the bookstore. But knowing all of that doesn't help me if my work isn't good. I may be a literary writer, but I still have to have a plot, and if I want people to read my work it's got to move at more than a snail's pace. Genre writers have the same bar. It's not like they can write a work that is devoid of similes and symbolism or setting. Even within the so-called subdivisions of the genre and literary worlds, things are mixed, procedurals often have elements of romance, there may be a satirical character in your tragedy.

Essentially good writing is just good writing no matter where it is shelved and what it is called. And good writing will have elements of many different devices, techniques, and styles, it will be varied. In fact, that's why I love my writing group, we each have a different identity: literary, horror, romance, sci-fi, which means we bring a different perspective to editing and critiques. Their input is crucial to make sure that I have a well-rounded piece, or in other words I need them to make sure what I have put out is "good," no matter the classification of the piece.

FROM THE "GENRE" AUTHOR:
A.E. SANTANA

I come from a career in marketing, communications, and public relations, so for me, the difference is marketing or, more accurately, publicity, which goes beyond paid advertisements and deals with how people perceive and talk about books. Some authors want to place a firm boundary between, say, Stephen King and Ernest Hemingway, although a reader may find both of their works sitting under "fiction" in a bookstore. So, let's go through some commonly stated interpretations of literary and genre, and see how each of these is more closely related to marketing/publicity (and societal bias) than it is to actual literary-ship.

Some people hold a strong belief that to be considered literary, a book must be carefully crafted with nuance, focusing on structure of sentence rather than structure of plot. How groundbreaking is the writing? How refined is the wording? On the other hand, people may believe that genre stories aren't written to push boundaries structurally and tend to use simpler prose.

But what of Stephen Graham Jones, whose horror novels are often critically acclaimed and labeled as "literary" horror? Or what of George Saunders, who is known as a literary author but whose works often slide into fantastical realms? If Jones and Saunders are both masters of the written word, writing nuanced, intellectual, and high-end prose with storylines and characters in outlandish and wondrous worlds—why is one's work "genre" and the other "literary"? Because they have been marketed that way. Where on the shelf do their books sit? Which circle of writers is talking about Jones? Which is talking about Saunders? How are book reviews labeling them? Which magazines, newspapers, journals write about them? Most importantly, where do they sell?

Perhaps it is not the writing style that marks the difference, or the content. As mentioned above, Jones and Saunders have both used fantastical story elements, and some great literary works like *A Christmas Carol* have "genre" elements like ghosts. Maybe then it is the purpose of the story. Is it meant to entertain? If so, some may be inclined to signal the story as genre. Genre stories are often seen as a place for escape and entertainment: romance, science fiction, high fantasy, etc. On the other hand, if the story is meant to give the reader a provocative and philosophical epiphany, then perhaps it's literary. Some people are equally inclined to say that literary stories are geared toward enrichment and include meaningful insight in some way.

Well, not exactly. It can be argued that all fiction is meant for entertainment. It can also be argued that genre stories often deal with provocative and philosophical ideals, and literary stories don't always have a meaning to take away. So, while readers may find books grouped together with those purposes for either genre or literary, it's not a hard and fast rule, and they're usually grouped that way for marketing purposes (where on the bookshelf, where do they sell, etc.).

Then maybe it is the plot or setting that marks the difference. In genre stories, readers may find plots with a strong external conflict. In literary stories, readers may find plots with strong internal conflict. But that's not a strict rule either; it's mostly another way that marketing has been able to bundle titles together to sell to the same reader. Also, while most literary stories don't take place in a medieval-type fantasy land or on strange planets or deep under the ocean, sometimes they do, think *The Time Machine* or *Twenty Thousand Leagues Under the Sea* (both science fiction but also literary classics). Then, some genre works take place in a small quaint town, and the best thing that ever happened there is two people fall in love—no magic, no spaceships, no dragons, or robots.

If we have two novels that have a similar writing style, plot, and purpose but one story is set in New York with troubled youth and one is set in outer space with rebellious teens, it still seems obvious that one is literary and one is genre. The New York story is going to sell better as a "moving, intellectual work of art," and the story set in outer space is going to sell better as an "action-packed, cosmic adventure."

However, advertisers didn't decide on these labels marooned on an island. They are based on audience perception and expectation. Maybe someone doesn't want to read a book with dragons and robots fighting subterranean aliens. Maybe someone doesn't want to read a book about the struggles of a guy down and out on his luck in northern Arizona. Maybe someone doesn't want to spend their time tackling complicated sentence structure. Maybe someone isn't interested in reading extended fight scenes. But maybe someone does. And if one person does, then other people do too. So begins the sifting of stories into categories for people to find the ones they want to read. From there, publishers use marketing and publicity strategies to help drive sales based on these interests.

Thus, the difference is marketing and publicity. The difference is what do audiences *want* to read, not which is better to read. I believe that's the crux of the matter; literary and genre labels are there to 1) drive sales and 2) help readers discover stories they are interested in (which helps drive sales). When we begin to give importance to one concept or label over the other is when things become muddled. So, when a genre book seems to be snubbed for the Pulitzer, that may have to do more with marketing/publicity than with the actual worth or craft of the book.

ABOUT A.M. LARKS

A.M. Larks writes fiction, nonfiction, children's literature, and drama. Her writing has appeared in *Scoundrel Time*, *Assay: A Journal of Nonfiction Studies*, *Five on the Fifth*, *Charge Magazine*, and the *Zyzzyva* and *Ploughshares* blogs. She has performed her stories at Lit Up at Town Hall Theatre in Lafayette, California. She is the current photo editor and blog editor at *Kelp Journal*, a multimedia literary revue, and the former fiction editor at *Please See Me* literary magazine as well as the former media editor of *The Coachella Review*.

A.M. Larks earned a Bachelor of Arts in English Literature, a Juris Doctorate, and most recently a Master of

Fine Arts in Creative Writing and Writing for the Performing Arts from the University California Riverside Palm Desert's low-residency program. She is a longtime patron of the arts and enjoys stories that capture the complexities of life on the page or screen.

About A.E. Santana

A.E. Santana is a Southern California native who grew up in a farming community surrounded by the Sonoran Desert. A lover of horror and fantasy, her works can be found in *Latinx Screams*, *Demonic Carnival III*, and other horror anthologies. She is the managing editor for Kelp Journal & Books. A.E. Santana is a member of the Horror Writers Association and has particpated in several horror panels, including "No Longer the Scream Queen: Women's Roles in Horror." She received her MFA in fiction from the University of California, Riverside's low-residency program. Her perfect day consists of a cup of black tea and her cat, Flynn Kermit. Discover more at aesantana.com. Twitter and Instagram: @foxflur

LIVING WITH CRAFT

by Maria Duarte

Growing up in mexico, I never had the opportunity to learn about being a writer. I read Sor Juana Ines de la Cruz's poems when I was studying there, and since then I knew I wanted to spend some of my time writing. But I did not know where to start, where to look for opportunities for me to learn about writing or know anyone that could teach me. Careers in the Arts In Mexico are not recommended to the lower socioeconomic population; this career choice is geared toward those who have economic stability and are able to dedicate time to the craft. Students of my socioeconomic level are always encouraged to study careers that are practical and that will leave more money in the pockets and that would assure you a job when the studies were done. I don't think my family took me seriously as a writer, a poet, until I graduated from my master's program and even then, they were skeptical that I would be able to make a living with this career choice.

It was in high school that I had the opportunity to even think about becoming a writer. The first years of high school in Long Beach, California, were spent learning a foreign language and getting acquainted with the culture. At the time, I was not worried too much about the career I was going to choose when I got to college or even if I was going to college, but my teacher from English Literature made a significant impact on those ideas. In her classroom, in the 900 building, I read *Jane Eyre*, and it was the first book I understood in which my brain could actually think in English instead of translating as we usually do when we are learning a second language. My teacher had taught me to make sense of the language in the book by paying attention to the details of the sentences, to see their structure, to be aware of the construction of the paragraph, to see the woven words in a page describing a scene. It was the first time I was aware of the magic words can make. And all of those elements of part of the craft of writing, but that's not necessarily what I'd like to discuss.

Craft—the art of making something. For me as a writer, the question is always to create or not to create? Mainly because I am always procrastinating until I know I am ready to start a conversation with the blank page. Not all writers need time to "cook" the idea in their head, so they can put it on the page and make sense of it. The fear, for me, is to allow myself to be who I truly am, vulnerable, with no inhibitions, and be able to share that with the world. Even though I might feel the need to write, I might not have the strength to do it. Most of the time, it feels like the moment after I have a climax: sensibly aware of all the items in the room, of the portraits on the walls, of the mistakes made in the past—the images flow like a roller coaster, and I am overwhelmed to the point of crying. I just noticed this while writing this essay; I cry every time I am done with a piece of writing, and that might be because it stays with me for so long, and when it is finally released, it is as if a weight had been lifted out of my soul. I remember reading Bukowski and how he would "cook" poems in his head until they were ready; without knowing this, I have been doing it all this time.

And you might ask, what does any of this—moving countries, learning a new language, worrying about a career—have to do with craft? Well, in learning about yourself, you learn your craft. With the territory of knowing myself comes knowing the methods that work for me to start writing and continue to write. I know when it is the right time and when it is not; I know when I have "cooked" the poem enough that it is ready to be written. I know when I must read something to learn something. To me, craft is learning how I, as a writer and as a person, work in this life, not just how to write. And I should say, as I learn more and more about my craft, craft also helps me discover the person I am becoming as I grow with the years.

My take on poetry is that it must feel authentic, it must come from that place that tells us to write, and we don't know why. Nowadays, everything is suspicious of being "real;" as writers, we cannot spill lines that are superfluous, artificial, fake, or too perfectly constructed, lines that are hard to believe and are stripped of the rawness of being human. I say this because in this age of technology a lot of art comes to us, the viewer, the reader, the recipient of information in an artificial way. I feel that as artists trying to connect in some way to our authentic selves, we have some responsibility to be honest and present works that transmit that honesty. The page deserves our honesty to pass it along to the reader through images that are made with a certain sentiment of sincerity. That certain sentiment of sincerity is our truth as beings that we share with anyone who reads our words. I do understand that we all have different perspectives, as we see life differently, but we have more in common than we may realize. There is a common humanness in our living, in our sharing this planet we call home, in our ecstasy of dying and our depression of living. I believe it is necessary to strip our nurture, to get in touch with our nature, our instinct to share our true self as honestly as possible.

In college, I chose a class with poet Frank Gaspar, and after that I did not look back on wanting to be a writer. I did not choose to be a writer, it was an innate necessity to use language as a form of expression, even though more times than not I find myself restricted by that language too. I was mistaken on what it would take to become a writer because even after I have received a master's degree I still do not feel like a true writer. This, I have come to discover, is because even though I want to write, I do not wish to be enslaved by it.

Let me explain:

Life is only one moment, time is infinite—in a way, it is all about balance. What works for me, might not work for someone else. I have molded my life for the lifestyle I live, which is that I have a main job and then I write on the side.

Writing takes so much out of me that to do this full time would probably send me into a depressed mode, because spiritually I would be so exhausted. I admire those who can sit for hours and write—and maybe it is discipline, but I cannot do it, it doesn't matter how much I try. I have learned that with time—and, believe me, I have had time to think about this—writing to me has been salvation, the shooting star that comes from time to time, but when it appears it renews not only my sense of self but my humanness as well. It is sporadically that I write. I read more. Writing is a physical activity where not only my mind is reacting to what I am writing but also my body. It overtakes me, it gives me ecstasy, but it also gives me the hell that comes after, and of that I cannot take a lot.

You see, there is always that desire to write more, to sit at the desk and write more, to capture all the words roaming around my mind on the blank page. But what if the words are not what the page expected? What if they are not good enough? What if I cannot write what I want to write and something else comes out? Those questions are always going to be there, but what really stops me is, in itself, life. Any craft requires time, it requires commitment, it requires the ability to stop living for some time and analyze the life I have been living. Being the overthinker that I am, I am already doing this with every decision I make I don't want writing, especially my poetry, to become less than the rawness of my being. I want my poetry to be free of the constructions that society has groomed me to believe while growing up and studying. I have discovered, by observing children, how we lose the awe-ness, the wonder in our later years. This inevitable gives us the excuse to put layers and layers of coverings on us that prohibits us form being true to who we are. I want the words written with my hand to feel, I want them to jump with emotion—so much perfection on the page takes away, for me, the beautiful imperfection that we *are*.

I remember reading about how Emily Dickinson wrote on all the scraps of paper she could find because it would take too much time to sit and write. For her, life was probably more important than properly sitting down and writing. That is how I feel; life should take the main seat in this journey, not only because we eventually run out of time to do what makes us happy, but because if it doesn't come out of the soul, I am not interested in writing about it.

I don't write because I have to for monetary reasons, or because I am obsessed with it, or because I will make a life with it and leave a legacy. I write because it renews my soul in a way no other activity can; it helps me understand not only myself but the environment in which I am living. It helps me discover the entrails of my being, the hidden messages of my bones, the pockets of air running through my veins from one part of my body to the other, it helps me paint my being into reality.

I usually have some type of alcohol in hand—and no I am not an alcoholic, and no it is not a trigger, and no I don't get drunk while writing. It is more of a relaxation technique for me; I am afraid of the blank page. Wow! I have never admitted that! I am afraid not only of the blank page, but I am also intimidated by the pureness of it. The blank page brings lucidity, what if I don't like it? What if it is too much to handle? Can lucidity make me crazy? I would not care if I were crazy, as long as it didn't hurt anyone else. But this life is more complicated, we are all intertwined in one way or another, so even when we are alone, we are never alone.

That is another thing writing has opened my eyes to, that even when we feel the loneliest, we are never truly alone. There is this invisible community of writers that have come before us and that have shared their gift with us, and that is something no one can take away. I have taken so many lessons from current and past writers, and even though I feel I can never finish learning, it has giving me the confidence to be who I am.

This is the one main point writing has made for me: We all have things to learn from this life and reading different writers from diverse backgrounds has taught me so much of what it really means to be alive and to be human. I think we forget to be humans from time to time because either we are not interested, or we are too wrapped up in our own world—we forget that we are not the only ones on this earth. Reading makes us aware of not only our environment but also of others and how they live. I believe all writing is valuable because it teaches us how people see the world and it teaches us of the different perspectives that we all have.

I have no shame in saying that my writing style will not be liked by many, but this is life—and like all writing—this is about perspective. My choice is to see the glass full rather than half empty because, after all, I am able to write whenever I want to write and to live all the time and enjoy it. I know writing can give us wings. I have traveled to so many distant places that I feel I know the world even though I have not physically been everywhere in it.

Sometimes, I do wish I could write like Fernando Pessoa or Cesar Vallejo; I wish I could describe beautiful things in the beautiful way in which they do so readers would be enamored with words, but the truth is that I probably do not write like that, and I never will. Fantasies rule the world. Even though this is a decent wish, and I hear a lot of new writers say this, I would not recommend writing like somebody else because then it would not be you writing but someone else.

Discover yourself, try different kinds of writing, learn as much as you can but take only what feels right for you, be honest, sincere with yourself. Touch the petal of a tulip, smell the orchids, dance until you cannot feel your feet, try all kinds of eggs, and decide which one you like best. Be you; in whatever form you want to be. Craft is an extension of who you are because you are the creator, learn about yourself, invest time in knowing who you are, and the writing will follow.

About Maria Duarte

Maria Duarte is a poet and writer who received her MFA in Creative Writing from the University of California, Riverside in Palm Desert. She has published poems in *Verdad Magazine* from Long Beach City College, in the anthology *The Good Grief Journal: A Journey Toward Healing* and a personal essay "Dear America" in *Air/Light Magazine*. She is currently the poetry editor for *Kelp Journal.*

ACKNOWLEDGEMENTS

First and foremost, I have to thank my editors past and present who contributed to this project: A.E. Santana, Chih Wang, A.M. Larks, Maria Duarte, and Leslie Gonzalez. *Kelp Journal* has grown so much over the past three years and none of it would be possible without you. All of the countless hours you all have spent keeping this magazine operating at peak levels is a testament to your dedication to the literary community, writing, and to craft. These essays are wonderful contributions to the craft cannon.

I also have to give a big, heartfelt thank you to Tod Goldberg and the UC Riverside, Palm Desert MFA. The Hottest MFA on the planet. This life changing low-residency program brought us all together and remains one of the greatest experiences of my life.

A big thank you to Jill French for her copy editing. Your careful eye has helped tremendously.

And last, a thank you to the readers and contributors of *Kelp Journal*. Thank you so much for helping us make the magazine something special. You mean the world to us.

— DAVID M. OLSEN